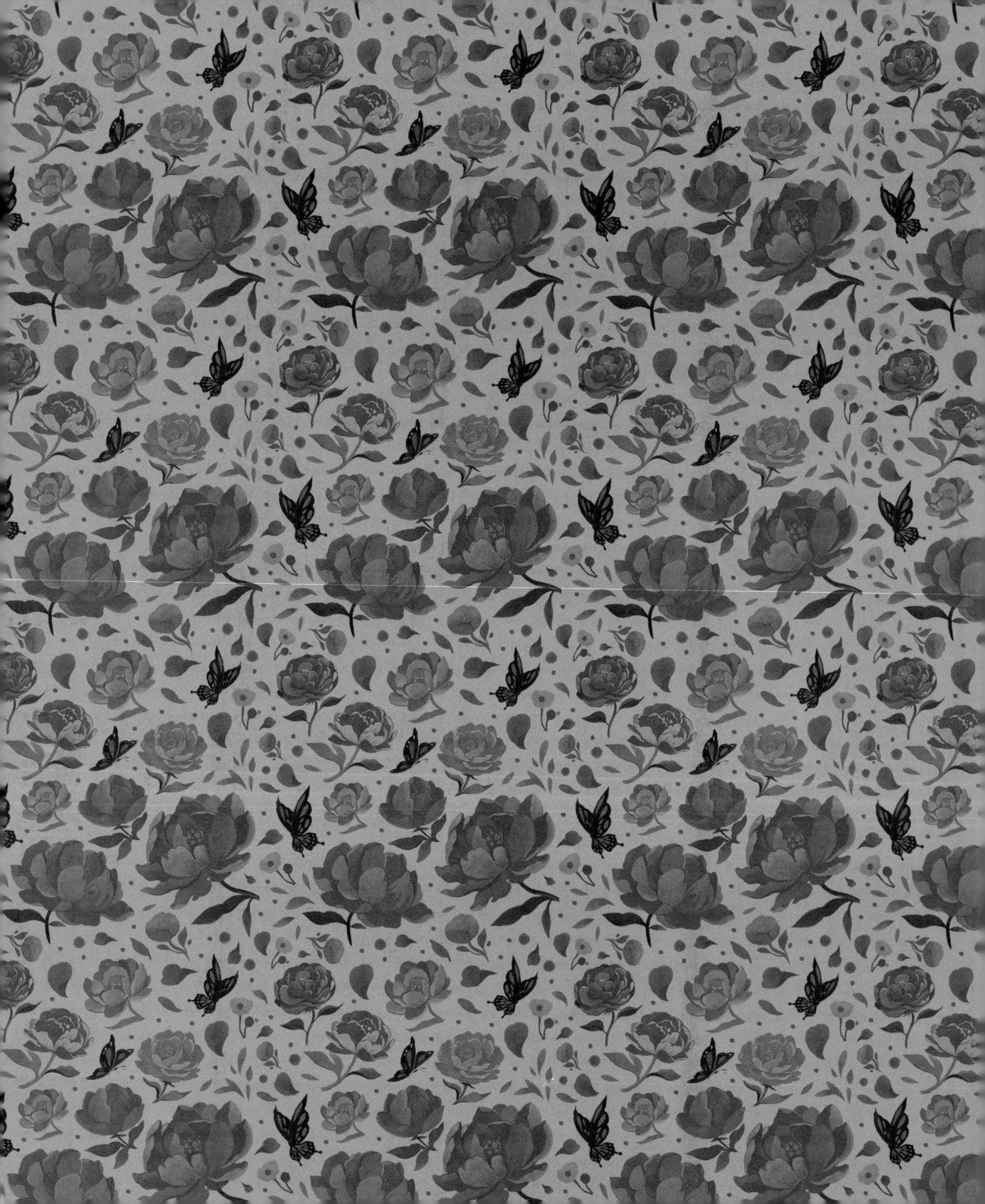

Enchanted Tales

For Chinelo,

with Love, Aunty Naomi
x X x

To Elia and Anna, who don't need me to tell them stories
are the best thing EVER … but who let me, anyway – L.S.

To my mom and my sister, who made me believe in fairy tales – L

A TEMPLAR BOOK

First published in the UK in 2023 by Templar Books,
an imprint of Bonnier Books UK,
4th Floor, Victoria House,
Bloomsbury Square, London WC1B 4DA
Owned by Bonnier Books
Sveavägen 56, Stockholm, Sweden
www.bonnierbooks.co.uk

1 3 5 7 9 10 8 6 4 2

ISBN 978-1-80078-591-5

This book was typeset in Garth Graphic Pro, Dulcinea and Scrivano
The illustrations were created with gouache, watercolour and digital mediums

Edited by Carly Blake, Emily Thomas
and Sophie Hallam
Designed by Chris Stanley
Production by Nick Read

Printed in China

Enchanted Tales

Written by Laura Sampson

Illustrated by Quang and Lien

templar
books

A Note From The Author

Enchantment, sorcery, curses, spells – *magic* – set the world of stories apart from our everyday lives. But tales of enchantment also help us notice the magical powers that exist in our own world, too – in our landscapes, the strength of our feelings and even in the things we say. After hearing, telling or reading an enchanted tale, life feels richer, stranger and more full of wonder.

There are, of course, lots of different kinds of enchantment, in lots of different places. In *Enchanted Tales* I've included stories from all over the world – a mix of short folk tales, epic quests, wonder tales and small sections of much bigger, longer myth stories. Each explores the power of magic: they tell of wishes granted, forest spirits, and magical worlds near and far, far away. There are witches and wizards, mischievous imps and journeys to the very end of the world. There are warm, loving stories for cuddling up to, where magic rewards kindness, alongside more complex tales of curses, nefarious plots and tests of strength – for those who feel brave enough to step into them.

Many of these stories have travelled long and complicated roads to reach our eyes and ears in today's world. Some are clearly inspired by one place, but written by someone from quite another. Others are from communities invaded and wronged by the very people who collected stories to tell to the rest of the world. Yet more appear in many versions in many countries, creating their own family of stories, which folklorists call 'tale types'. Sometimes, the magnificent stories that make up this book have managed to reach us against all odds. Reading them, hearing them told and (most importantly) telling them to others will help their magic live on in our hearts.

Laura Sampson

Contents

Lotus Cloud Mountain
A tale from Vietnam

Stepping into an enchanted kingdom is one of the most magical things ever. It happens in stories from all over the world: in the Japanese story of Urashima Taro, a kind boy visits a spectacular undersea kingdom; in the Irish story of Oisin, a hero visits a land where everyone lives forever. In "Lotus Cloud Mountain", the magical kingdom hovers on top of water, and the whole story is filled with the sweet fragrance of flowers.

A long, long time ago, in the bustling district of Tien Du, by the flat, green floodplains of Bac Ninh province, lived a young man named Tu Thuc. He was kind, clever and liked by everybody. In his job as District Chief – the youngest in the province – he solved disputes, organised festivals and made important decisions. But every night, he dreamed of a blissful land beyond the clouds, full of sweet aromas and beautiful flowers from ancient stories.

It was the season of the red peony blossom festival – Tu Thuc's favourite time of year. The Phat Nanh pagoda gardens were filled with bushes heavy with the beautiful blooms. Tu Thuc went to see them and marvelled at the piles of petals along every walkway, but as he breathed in their wonderful scent, he heard voices shouting:

"Stop thief! No flower-picking! Vandal! You'll pay!"

"I didn't mean to! The branch broke!"

Tu Thuc turned and saw security guards holding onto a young woman, exquisite as a lotus flower. Without stopping to think, Tu Thuc took off his coat.

"Guards, release her! This is clearly an unfortunate accident. Take this coat as payment for the damage," he said.

The young woman smiled at Tu Thuc, bowed low and hurried away.

Tu Thuc returned to his duties. Days passed, and he worked hard as ever, but he could not forget the young woman he had helped at the pagoda. She reminded him of his dream. Soon, all he could think about was escaping the routine of town and work, to travel and see the beauty of the world – maybe the blissful land itself!

Finally, he did it – he left his job and started walking. With land on one side and sea on the other, Tu Thuc passed mountains of pink marble, emerald-green waters and magnificent caves. One evening, at sunset, he looked across the sea to the horizon. A group of clouds seemed to hover there above the surface, unfolding like lotus flowers. A vision of the young woman at the flower festival appeared in his mind stronger than ever.

Without stopping to think, Tu Thuc ran to the water's edge, climbed into a boat and began rowing out towards the lotus-clouds. As he got closer, he realised the clouds were not clouds at all, but an island! Huge pearly cliffs rose up from the ocean. Were they real? Tu Thuc reached out his hand and touched a smooth surface – it *felt* real! Suddenly a small passageway opened before him in the cliff, and a strong fragrance of flowers wafted from it. Delighted, Tu Thuc breathed in: "Ah! The flowers from my dreams!"

Leaving the boat behind, he followed the direction of the scent until he reached a magnificent room, glowing with light and rainbow colours. Piles of flowers of all kinds – peonies, peach blossoms, phoenix flowers, marigolds – filled the space. The floor was strewn with petals and the air rang with voices singing to welcome him. At the end of the room was a throne, where a figure sat dressed in the ornate woven robes of a queen, and, beside her, the young woman from the flower festival!

"Welcome, Tu Thuc of the earthly realm of dust and shadows. We have long awaited your arrival! Do you know where you are?" asked the queen.

Tu Thuc bowed politely. "Madam, I am overwhelmed and overjoyed by the beauty of this place, but I do not know its name. Please tell me and I will shout it to the world!"

"You are in the sixth of the thirty-six grottoes of Lotus Cloud Mountain – your kind might call it 'fairyland'. Our land floats above the ocean, but never touches it, and travels where it will. I am Nguy, queen of this place. Your kindness saved my daughter, Giang Huong. Your heart is noble. You are welcome here."

Giang Huong stepped forward to speak. Her voice rang in Tu Thuc's heart. "You helped me in the pagoda garden, and since then I have longed to see you again. If you are willing, we will be married here."

"It was you I left my home to find. I wish to be with you always."

Instantly, there was a royal wedding. Music and laughter filled the air, delicious food and drink appeared on tables and the new bride and groom began their life together. Each day after was happier than the next for Tu Thuc and Giang Huong in Lotus Cloud Mountain.

One day, after almost a year, Tu Thuc was sitting near the mountain entrance when the lotus cloud cliffs parted. He glimpsed outside and saw a familiar boat – *That's just like the one I rowed here in!* he thought – and the distant shore from where he had first seen the lotus clouds. Suddenly he remembered his home, his district – the people he knew. How long had he been away? Panicked, he ran straight to Giang Huong to explain.

"My love, I hate to leave you even for a moment, but I must return home to Tien Du, and let my friends and relatives know I am well. I cannot rest until I do."

Giang Huong's sparkling eyes became serious. "My love, I understand your heart's wish. But life is short. If you go, it may not be so easy to return; Lotus Cloud Mountain goes where it will. You might not find me."

"Never! My heart led me here, to you – it can lead me here again."

"If you must return, my love goes with you. Come. This time, you will not travel by boat." Giang Huong clapped her hands and a carriage of lotus clouds appeared. Tu Thuc climbed in. "Now close your eyes," she said.

In one blink of Tu Thuc's eyes, the carriage flew from Lotus Cloud Mountain and landed on the outskirts of Tien Du district. He was home! But although the pagoda and peony bushes were still there, Tu Thuc saw nobody he recognised.

"How strange!" Tu Thuc said to himself. He sat down, not sure what to do, as a very old man was passing by.

"Who do you seek? You look lost," asked the old man.

"I am Tu Thuc, I have been away but came back to my birthplace."

"Tu Thuc, you say? I am the record keeper here and nobody by that name has lived here in over 300 years! Tu Thuc was a young official who was very popular, but he disappeared one day and never came back. Are you sure that is your name, sir?"

At once, Tu Thuc understood. It was like the old stories said, time passes differently in places like Lotus Cloud Mountain. For each day there, one year had gone by here.

"Everything I know is gone," Tu Thuc wept. "I must go home to Giang Huong."

He turned to step back into the lotus cloud carriage – it had disappeared! But Tu Thuc did not despair. He knew that his heart would lead him to Giang Huong. He set off along the coast, following his heart's path, to find Lotus Cloud Mountain. One day, he may find it again.

Under the Iroko Tree
A Yoruba tale from West Africa

The Iroko tree is a tall spreading tree with silver bark and shiny, dark green leaves, which can live for more than 500 years. It is found in the tropical forests of West Africa, and features in stories of magic, mystery and luck. In some Yoruba myths, a trickster spirit lives inside the tree. Some people believe it is very bad luck to cut the tree down, because the spirits of their ancestors watch over them from the inside.

Long ago in a country of hot sun and red earth, there lived a Hunter who was very unlucky. Every day he went into the forest to hunt for food to fill his belly and to sell at the market, but he never caught a thing, so he went home with empty pockets and an even emptier belly.

"All the animals seem to hide when they see me coming!" the Hunter sighed in despair, as he strapped his bow and arrows onto his back and trudged through the forest towards home.

In the forest there was a great Iroko tree, whose silver

trunk rose up from red earth to branches brimming with shining leaves like outstretched arms. One afternoon, tired, hungry and sad after another unlucky day, the Hunter sat with his back against the Iroko tree's trunk and his head in his hands.

"What shall I do? Tell me, what shall I do?" the Hunter's voice echoed from tree to tree. Just then he heard a rustle of leaves and looked up to find an old woman in a long robe made of tree-bark, staring down at him with unblinking eyes. She was tall and stern, with long, thin hands.

"Do not lose hope, young man. Things are never as bad as they seem," she said. Then the Old Woman commanded, "Give me your weapons, give me your clothes and climb this tree. Do it now!"

Huh? the Hunter thought, but he obeyed and climbed to the top of the tree and peered down. The ground was a long way away.

"Now, Hunter," called the Old Woman, "you must hang upside down, let go and fall to the ground."

Huh? This is crazy! thought the Hunter. *But I suppose I have nothing to lose.* He counted down – *three, two, one* – and then let go. The moment he hit the ground the world disappeared.

All of sudden there was sound – commotion! Strange noises reached the Hunter's ears – wheels turning, footsteps scurrying and voices shouting:

"Your Majesty?! Your Majesty?!"

How strange! he thought. *Such noises do not belong in the deep forest. And why are people shouting "Your Majesty"?*

Still lying on the ground, he opened his eyes. He gasped. This was not the forest. This was a highway! Hooves, wheels and shoes were passing through pattern-carved city gates. "Where am I?" the Hunter demanded.

"Your Majesty! You're awake!" A crowd of worried-looking people in servants' uniforms cheered.

The Hunter looked around and behind him, completely confused. *They can't mean me?* he thought. But they did. They picked the Hunter up and placed him in a fine carriage, where fine robes were waiting for him. The carriage began to move and, before long, clattered into the city. It passed crowds of cheering people, heading towards a grand palace.

The Hunter was led inside to the throne room where 101 royal crowns sat on 101 plinths, and gold, jewels and precious things from all over the world lined the walls. A crown was selected and placed on his head and the Hunter was crowned king.

Wise advisors walked the palace with the confused King and explained: "All this is yours, Your Majesty. All except one thing. There." They pointed to a tiny door in a tiny wall. "This is the door of *'Too Much Too Soon'* – if you want to keep what you have, NEVER open it!" Awestruck by all the riches, the Hunter-King agreed and his reign began.

Days, weeks and months passed. The Hunter-King ruled wisely and well. There was always plenty of food to eat. People came from far and wide to visit him. He was so busy with his royal duties he forgot all about the door of *"Too Much Too Soon"*.

Before long, a year had flown by, and preparations for a Jubilee party to celebrate the Hunter-King's reign began. Artists and engineers made huge paper lanterns to parade through the city in his honour and the whole kingdom was invited to a feast.

On the day of the Jubilee party, tables were piled high with delicious things to eat and drink. There was talking and music and dancing. Every guest gave the Hunter-King gifts, and praised him for his wisdom, style and power. Delighted with his first royal celebration, the Hunter-King ate, drank, danced and talked until late into the night.

Finally, the last guest left. The Hunter-King was alone in the throne room and the tiny door caught his eye. He remembered what his wise advisors had told him. "But that was then. This is MY kingdom, MY door, and I can open it if I want!" declared the Hunter-King out loud to the empty room. He turned the handle, opened the door and squeezed through.

"Hunter, back so soon?" said a familiar voice.

Lying on the ground under the Iroko tree, the Hunter looked around him – it was as if he had never been gone. The sun shone through the leaves of the Iroko tree onto the face of the Old Woman, who handed him his clothes and his bow and arrows.

"There are some doors that, if opened, cannot be closed again," said the Old Woman. "But do not lose hope, young man, things are never as bad as they seem. You live and learn." And then she was gone.

The Little Stars of Gold
A tale from Czechia

Have you ever noticed that being kind to others makes you feel good, too? In this story, a young girl's actions bring a little bit of magic to those she meets, and in turn she receives a magical reward. In the past, many of the people who shared folk tales owned very little: perhaps they looked up at the night sky, and imagined how wonderful it would be if the sparkling stars could send some magic their way...

Long ago, a little orphan girl named Magda lived with her godfather in a tiny house beside a forest. Magda had a quick mind and a warm heart, and though she and Godfather didn't have much, they were happy.

One autumn morning, Godfather said, "Little Magda! Today I must go on a long journey, and I cannot take you with me. You must go through the forest to stay with your aunt. It is not so very far. Can you make your way alone?"

"Yes, Godfather," said Magda.

"I will return soon," he promised.

Autumn days were chilly, so Magda dressed warmly and set out on her way. She carried only the clothes she wore and a small bundle of food for the journey, with her godfather's large black silk handkerchief in her skirt pocket.

Along the winding path, dry leaves crunched under Magda's feet. Nobody else was around and it seemed she was the only person in the world, until – oh! Magda heard a cough. Beside the road, wrapped in faded rags, was an old man with a long grey beard, so thin he looked as though he could have blown away.

"Girl! Got any food?" he croaked. Magda was already opening her bundle.

"I'm Magda," she said. "I would be pleased if you'd share a meal with me." She sat down beside the old man, and together they ate and drank. The old man smiled.

"Thank you, kind one – may your journey be short and paved with stars of gold!" he said.

"Blessings on you." Magda retied her bundle and continued along the winding path, with the sun shining its final rays through the trees.

But then – oh! From under a great oak tree, came a sound. A sob. Someone was crying! Magda looked down. There between the roots, a little girl with red hair was curled up, small as a squirrel. She was shivering in the chilly autumn air because she had no coat.

The red-haired girl looked up at Magda. "Sister! Sister! Won't you help me get warm?"

"Here." Magda unbuttoned her winter coat, with its fleecy lining, and gave it to the girl. "My journey is not far. You will be warmer now."

The red-haired girl stopped crying, put on the coat and smiled up at Magda. "Thank you for your kindness – may your way be marked with sparkles!"

Magda thanked her and continued on. Sunset became blue twilight and the air was still... But – oh! Another sound. There, by a chattering stream, sat a

young dark-eyed woman, humming in a deep voice as she tried to sew fallen leaves together to make a skirt, because hers was full of holes.

"Excuse me." Magda unravelled the long, wide blanket-scarf from around her neck. "Please, take this, and wear it however you like," she told the woman. "My mother always said that love is in the stitches."

"You are very kind. I will treasure this," the woman said. "May your travels be lit by starlight, Sister!"

Again Magda walked on, and soon twilight became darkness. But, then – oh! Movement! Light! The air above Magda grew warm, as though a giant candle had been lit by an unseen hand. And there, from the sky, shimmering gold flecks floated down. Magda thought they must be fireflies. But they were stars!

"How beautiful!" said Magda. From her skirt pocket she took out her godfather's handkerchief to catch the stars as they fell, and one by one, they led her to the house of her aunt, who threw open the door in welcome.

"Come in! It's late," she said. "To bed! We'll talk in the morning!"

Tired, Magda slept soundly but woke early to help her aunt.

"My dear," said her aunt, inspecting the large black silk handkerchief. "I expected you to come with nothing. But this handkerchief seems full of something. What's inside?"

"Stars!" said Magda, pulling at the handkerchief's corners. But instead, she found gold and silver coins – enough for Magda and her aunt to live comfortably until Godfather returned. Maybe even longer. "But we can't just keep them," she said. "These are gifts – we must share them!"

"A wise choice," said her aunt, nodding.

Together, they sat down at the kitchen table and talked about who they could help next.

The Twelve Dancing Princesses
A tale from France by Charles Deulin

How enchanting it would be to open a door and step through into a secret world built especially for you! The twelve dancing princesses of this tale can do just that – a good reason why the story remains so popular across Europe, in lots of different versions. This one is by Charles Deulin, a French writer from a small town on the French-Belgian border, and is full of details – food, clothes and place names – inspired by his home region.

In the village of Montignies-sur-Roc lived a young cowherd named Michel. He had curly hair and pretty blue eyes, and people called him "Stargazer" because he was always gazing upwards, dreaming of adventures. One summer's day, a fairy in a golden dress appeared to him and sang, "Go to the Château of Beloeil, and you will marry a princess!"

The Stargazer eagerly did as the fairy instructed. When he arrived at the château the next day, everyone was talking about a strange mystery. Each night,

19

the twelve beautiful princesses of Beloeil went to bed in a suite of rooms locked with three strong bolts. But each morning, their satin shoes were worn through as if they had been dancing all night. Their father, the duke, had declared: "ANYONE WHO CAN SOLVE THE MYSTERY OF THE WORN-OUT SHOES MAY MARRY ONE OF MY DAUGHTERS!"

Princes had come from across the land to try their luck, but each one who came vanished overnight.

I am no prince – the duke will laugh at me if I come forward, thought Michel, so he found work in the château gardens, making daily bouquets for the princesses, who accepted them but never looked at him or thanked him.

But one day, the youngest, Lina, glanced up and smiled. Michel's heart leapt, and he longed to get to the bottom of the mystery.

That night the fairy appeared to Michel again with two baby laurel trees – a rose and a cherry – a golden bucket and a golden rake.

"Plant these laurel trees, tend them with this rake, water them from this bucket and they will grant your wishes!" she sang, before disappearing. Michel did as the fairy instructed.

One day the cherry bloomed with a white flower. Michel plucked the flower and placed it in his shirt button, hoping to impress the young princess. Miraculously, the flower instantly made Michel invisible! *This is my chance to solve the princesses' mystery!* he thought. That evening, invisible, he hid under a bed in their suite. As soon as the door was shut for the night, he heard wardrobes opening, clothes rustling and laughter. Then – CLAP! CLAP! CLAP! CREAK!

A trapdoor in the floor swung open. Michel slipped out from under the bed and followed the princesses through the door, so close he accidentally stepped on Lina's dress.

Lina looked behind her but saw nothing. "I must have tripped!"

Michel followed the princesses down a staircase, along a corridor, through a woodland of silver, then one of gold, and another of sparkling diamonds, until they came to a glass-clear lake. Twelve princes were waiting in twelve shining boats to row each princess across to a castle, which shone in the twilight. Michel sat invisible beside Lina.

Why is my boat so slow and heavy? she wondered. But the wild music coming from the castle soon distracted her.

The boats docked, and everybody rushed to the castle's ballroom. It was full of mirrors, sparkling lights and rich hangings. From a corner, Michel admired the dancing princesses. Lina's velvet-black eyes shone as she whirled across the jewelled dancefloor. He envied the princes dancing with them, not knowing that they were the suitors who had gone before: an enchanted potion had made them forget everything of the world above.

When the princesses' shoes were worn through, the music stopped and they ate sugar cookies, waffles and cakes. Then, Michel followed the princesses silently, back across the lake and through the diamond and gold woodlands.

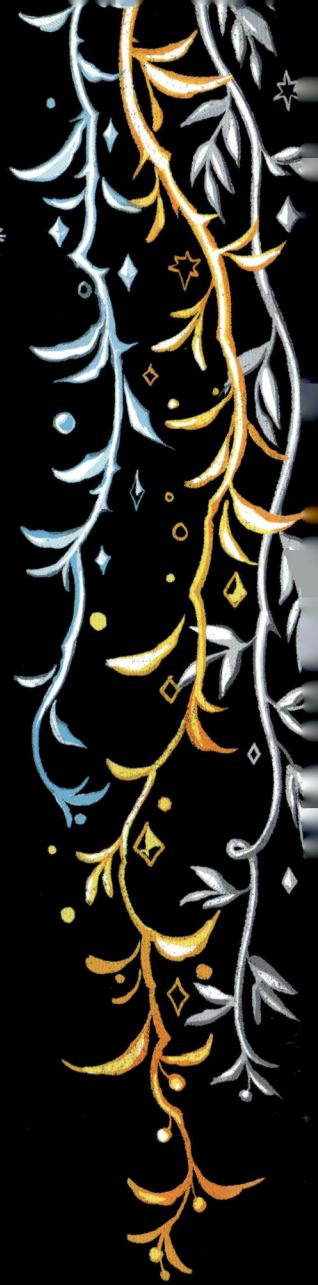

But at the silver woodland, he broke off a tiny sprig from one of the trees and – CLANG! – the whole wood rang.

"What was that?" asked one princess.

"Probably just a bird," said another.

Michel raced ahead to the princesses' suite – up the stairs, through the trapdoor, out of an open window and down a hanging vine back to the gardens at first dawn light. He removed the white invisibility flower and got to work gathering the princesses' daily bouquets. When Michel gave them to the princesses later, Lina found a silver twig in hers.

How can this be? she thought but said nothing.

For the next two nights Michel followed the princesses. Each time, on the way back, he plucked a sprig from a tree for Lina's bouquet – the next from the golden woodland and then from the diamond. When Lina found the diamond sprig, she confronted Michel. "You must have followed us. How?"

"I hid," Michel replied.

"You know that telling our father this secret rewards you with a wedding to one of us. Will you tell him?"

"I do not intend to," he replied.

"But why stay silent?" she asked, puzzled.

Michel said nothing, but the other princesses saw his blue eyes meet Lina's. They saw her heart melt.

"How ridiculous! Lina wants to be a gardener's wife!" they taunted.

"Never!" Lina cried and threw her bouquet at Michel with disdain.

Later that day, the sisters agreed that Michel should meet the same fate as the other suitors. They invited Michel to join them in plain sight that night.

Michel accepted, but he couldn't go to a grand dance dressed in his simple clothes. Then he remembered the rose laurel. In the gardens, he

whispered a wish into its petals and, within a moment, he was dressed like a prince, in black velvet that matched Lina's eyes, and a diamond feather brooch sparkling on his cap.

Once again, through the trapdoor, down the stairs, through the woodlands of silver, gold and diamond, and towards the dance they went. Lina looked at Michel and laughed, embarrassed. "Don't you look princely!" she said.

"Maybe. But I'm still a gardener," he said. "Not good enough for you."

They danced all night, and when the ball was over, the eldest princess held out a golden cup, and said, "Gardener, secret-revealer, let's drink to you!"

Michel had overheard them talking and knew the cup contained the forgetting potion, but he took it and raised it to his lips anyway, with a longing look at Lina.

"NO!" Lina cried. She ran to him and seized the cup before he could drink. "Gardener or not, the thought of you trapped here forever breaks my heart!" True love broke the spell for everyone. Together, they returned to the world above and closed the trapdoor, which disappeared forever.

In the Duke of Beloeil's private quarters, Michel told him everything, and asked for Lina's hand in marriage. The wedding was the biggest and happiest in the land, and Michel became a prince. He never needed to wish on the two laurels again because he had everything he could ever desire.

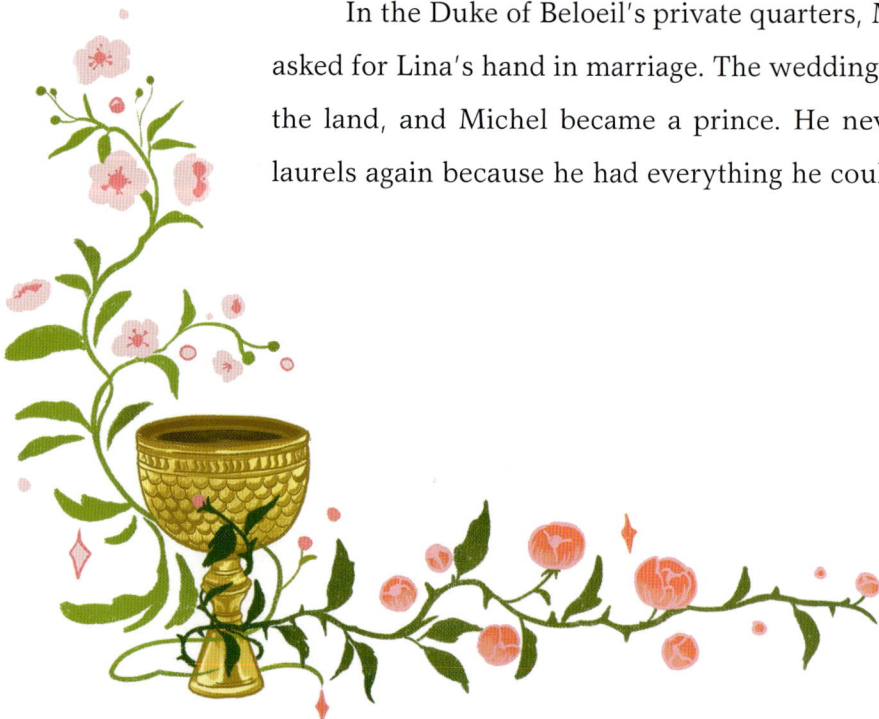

Sigurd and Fafnir
A tale from Scandinavia

In stories from Northern Europe and Scandinavia, dragons and serpents are famous for their cunning, their magic, and how much they love to hoard gold and treasure. But they can be wise, too, sometimes giving the hero of a story advice – even in the middle of a fight! In this thrilling episode from a famous legendary saga, a hero, with help from a Norse god in disguise, meets a notorious dragon for the first and last time.

In days gone by, there lived a young prince with piercing eyes named Sigurd. He grew up strong, fast and clever, brought up by his foster father, Regin, who he loved best in the world. Regin knew everything. He taught Sigurd many things – chess, languages and the secret symbols of rune magic, but what Sigurd loved most was a story that Regin told him every night, always the same:

In the beginning were Hreidmar and his three sons: Fafnir, who loved to own things; Otr, who swam, quick as water itself, in the form of an otter; and Regin, who was

25

always hungry for knowledge. One day, Odin and Loki – two gods of Asgard – came by the river to hunt. Loki killed and skinned an otter not knowing it was Otr, Hreidmar's son. Hreidmar demanded compensation in gold – enough to fill Otr's empty skin. Loki did as commanded but among that gold was a cursed ring, which Fafnir wanted to own so badly, it poisoned his mind. He killed his father, took the gold and hid it far away, where he guards it to this day, in dragon form.

One night, Regin turned to Sigurd and said, "Son, let us find that stolen gold and punish the thief!"

"But it's just a story!" Sigurd laughed, but Regin was serious.

"Sigurd, it is *my* story. I am as old as time. Fafnir is my brother. He took gold that was not his to take. You are strong, fast and clever – help me get it back!"

Sigurd stood and nodded. "I will, but first I must have a horse and a sword worthy of the task."

"You will have them," Regin replied.

Under a fire-red dawn sky the next morning, an old man with a long beard emerged from the birch forest surrounding Regin's house. His one eye shone as bright as three, and he led a huge grey horse.

"This is Grani," he said. "Grandson of Sleipnir, Odin's own horse. He is the best of horses and will never fail you."

With one look, Sigurd knew this was the perfect horse. He turned to thank the Old Man – but he was already gone.

Regin set to work in his forge, heating and hammering hot sword metal. His skill was unmatched, but still, he could not forge a sword strong enough for the quest. Then he remembered Gram, the sword broken in battle long ago by Sigurd's first father.

Sigurd found the pieces and with them Regin forged a sword strong enough to cut stone.

"Now, are you ready?" said Regin.

"I am," said Sigurd.

Together, they rode past mirror-still fjords and evergreen forests, until they came to a hill scarred with wide furrows. The trees were bare, no plants grew and the air was empty of birdsong. The bottom of the hill dropped steep as a cliff down to a broad lake.

"This hill is Gnitaheath," said Regin. "Here, Fafnir sits on the treasure that should be mine. He comes down to the lake to drink every day. Those furrows in the ground are his tracks. You must set a trap, Sigurd. Climb the hill, dig a deep trench in one of the furrows and wait. When Fafnir passes above, thrust the blade upwards and end him!" Regin's eyes glittered as if he could already see the hidden gold.

Sigurd took a breath: he could not turn back now, "Let's go, Foster Father."

"Not me. I will wait here." Regin passed Sigurd a shovel.

In the still grey air, without saying a word, Sigurd turned and climbed the hill. When he reached a large furrow, he dug a trench as wide and deep as a grave. As he stood at the bottom, he heard a voice behind him.

"Is this your trench?"

"Yes," Sigurd replied in surprise, turning round to face an old man with a long beard and one eye.

"You think this will save you from Fafnir? Think again if you want to live," said the Old Man. "Dig deeper, dig a slope and dig other trenches off this one, so you don't drown in poison. Do it now!"

"Who are you?" Sigurd questioned.

"Never mind names. Dig. Now."

The Old Man was stronger than he looked. They worked together, and soon the trench was bigger and deeper, with a network of smaller trenches. Sigurd turned to thank the Old Man but he was gone.

At that moment, the hill's peak seemed to unfurl – it was not rock but the giant serpent, Fafnir! The fearsome dragon spiralled down the hill, his poison-skin dissolving rock. The air shook. Fafnir drew nearer.

Sigurd jumped into the main trench, his back to the earth wall, and waited as the hill shivered and shook around him. Suddenly the trench went dark. Fafnir was above! Sigurd grasped his sword and thrust it upwards. It sliced through scales and skin to the dragon's heart. Poison-blood poured into the trench but drained away from Sigurd along the smaller trenches, just as the Old Man had said. Then there was light again.

Sigurd jumped out of the trench as a wounded Fafnir swung round to face him. "My slayer! Tell me your name!" he demanded.

Sigurd stood still. "I am Sigurd, foster son of Regin, the brother you wronged. For him, I take your gold and your life."

"Hah! Regin. I know him. He is a coward and a friend only to himself.

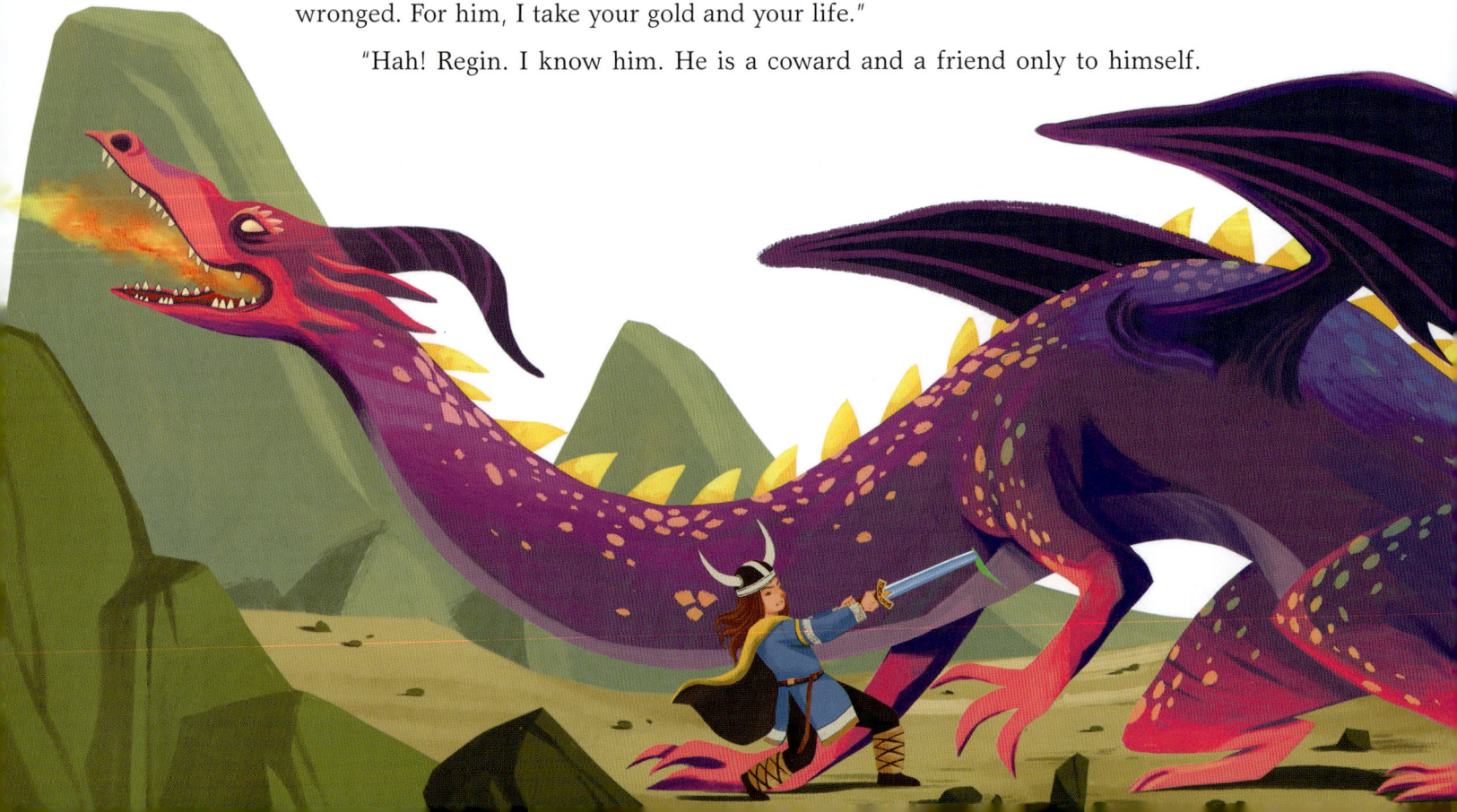

He cares nothing for you," Fafnir writhed and his breath rasped. "On this hill is more gold than you could ever spend. But know this – the gold is cursed, and it will cause your death!"

"Nobody escapes death," replied Sigurd.

As Fafnir died, Sigurd looked up the hill and saw the gold. It shone like bright dawn and reflected in his eyes. Then the shadow of Regin passed before him and he stood looking, too.

"Hail, winner of a great victory. The gold is ours now. And my brother is dead," Regin exclaimed.

Sigurd looked over at his beloved foster father and wondered if Fafnir's words were true.

"Foster Father, I kept my promise to you. What now?"

"Roast the dragon's heart and give it to me," Regin smiled.

Sigurd obeyed. He made a fire beneath a dead tree, cut out the dragon's heart and roasted it. Three birds landed above and watched in the tree's branches, chirping loudly. While the heart cooked, the juices spat and landed on Sigurd's finger – hot! He stuck his finger in his mouth and as the juice touched his tongue, the chirping of the birds became words:

"Roast dragon's heart means wisdom!"
"Take Regin's head, before Regin takes yours!"
"Sigurd should eat it, not the betrayer!"

Sigurd sat, listening to the birds and watching Regin. Now he had the wisdom of the dragon's heart – what he did with it is another story.

The Magic Fish

A tale from China

The Brothers Grimm version of "Cinderella" is the one many of us are familiar with, but there are hundreds – maybe even thousands – of different versions of this tale from around the globe. This version from China was the first to be written down, over 1,000 years ago.

Once upon a time, in a little shed outside a little house in the cave mountains of Southern China, there lived an orphan called Ye-Tsien. She was bright-eyed, clever, kind and good at making things. Ye-Tsien's stepmother loved her own daughter best, so Ye-Tsien had to do all the heaviest, most dangerous work, like collecting firewood from the deep forest or water from the high mountain pools.

One day, Ye-Tsien was collecting water when up from the bottom of a deep mountain pool there was a shimmering and a glittering. It travelled up and up until something broke the surface – a tiny, shining, golden fish! The fish looked up at Ye-Tsien, Ye-Tsien looked back – and from that moment, the fish and Ye-Tsien became friends. She took it home, placed it in a basin and fed it every day with scraps from her own plate. The fish grew and grew until, one day, it had grown so big she had to take it back to the pool. Still, Ye-Tsien visited the golden fish every day, and each time the fish would poke its shining golden head out of the water and greet her.

A few weeks later, the Stepmother was hungry and had an idea. Secretly, she followed Ye-Tsien to the pool. She saw how the huge, sparkling, delicious-looking fish always came out for Ye-Tsien but stayed deep under the water when anyone else came by. *How can I outwit this clever fish?* she thought.

The next day, back at home, the Stepmother gave Ye-Tsien new clothes to put on and sent her on a long errand down the mountain. Then she disguised herself in Ye-Tsien's old clothes, went to the pool and called the fish. When it bubbled up from the bottom of the pool, the Stepmother was ready with a knife. She took the golden fish home, chopped it up, cooked it and served it up to eat with her favourite daughter.

"Delicious!" they both said, wiping their mouths. They ate every morsel and threw its bones away on the rubbish heap.

The following day, Ye-Tsien hurried to the mountain pool and called – but no fish came. Big tears fell from her eyes and splashed into the empty pool. But as she cried, the air thickened, shimmering and glittering, and a figure appeared. It spoke in a voice that reminded her of safety:

> *Today you cry, today you weep,*
> *But look upon the rubbish heap.*
> *Your fish friend's magic bones are there.*
> *They'll grant you wishes, never fear.*

Then the figure disappeared. Ye-Tsien dried her cheeks, ran home and gathered the bones of the golden fish from the rubbish heap. She hid them in the woodpile but made no wish. Not until the first day of winter – the day of the Great Festival of the Ancestors. Ye-Tsien had never been before.

"Can I come to the festival with you, Mother?" Ye-Tsien asked.

"Absolutely not!" shouted the Stepmother. "You will stay here and chop this wood. Make sure you're finished by the time my daughter and I return!"

Alone again, Ye-Tsien wept into the woodpile. Then she remembered the hidden enchanted bones. Ye-Tsien carefully took them out and made a wish.

From the depths of the woodpile there was a shimmering and a glittering, and before her appeared an exquisite robe of kingfisher-blue feathers that shone with their own light and a pair of shoes woven from the finest threads of gold, with soles so soft they made no sound when she walked. As soon as Ye-Tsien put the robe and shoes on, she found herself at the festival! Crowds of people, delicious smells and colourful processions – Ye-Tsien was excited! Then, through the noise, Ye-Tsien heard a voice she recognised.

"Ye-Tsien, is that you?" her stepmother's voice rang out.

Stepmother can't find me here, Ye-Tsien thought. *I must get home before she finds out!* Ye-Tsien ran – past the stalls, past the processions, through the crowds – in the direction of the cave mountains; too fast to notice one golden shoe had fallen off her foot.

A passerby noticed it in the dust and gave it to their father, who gave it to a shoemaker, who sold it to a merchant, who took it to a palace on a great island far across the sea, where there lived a king who collected beautiful shoes.

"A shoe woven from the finest threads of gold, with soles so soft they make no sound!" the King said, admiring the glittering object. "But why just one? It is so exquisite, its wearer must be even more so. Find me the person this shoe fits!"

The King's advisors went around the island and made sure every single person tried on the shoe. But however small or big, long or thin, short or fat their feet were, none were the right shape or size to fit the golden shoe.

"There's only one thing for it. We must take the shoe back to where it was found and we won't return without its owner," the King declared.

Back across the sea at the cave mountains, the King's guards placed the shoe on the road, and hid. Soon, a young girl in ragged clothes carrying a bucket of water stopped in front of the shoe, gasped and picked it up. The guards followed her to a little shed outside a little house.

"Look! The other shoe!" one guard said, peering through the window.

"And a kingfisher-blue cloak fit for a queen!" the second guard said with surprise. "The girl must be a thief!"

Of course, Ye-Tsien wasn't a thief. When the guards brought her in front of the King, she told them the whole story about the golden fish, the magic bones and the wishes.

"WISHES?!" spluttered the King. "Even more interesting than beautiful shoes!" So the King asked Ye-Tsien to marry him.

"Of course she will!" said the Stepmother. There was a grand wedding and the King took Ye-Tsien, the golden shoes, the cloak and the

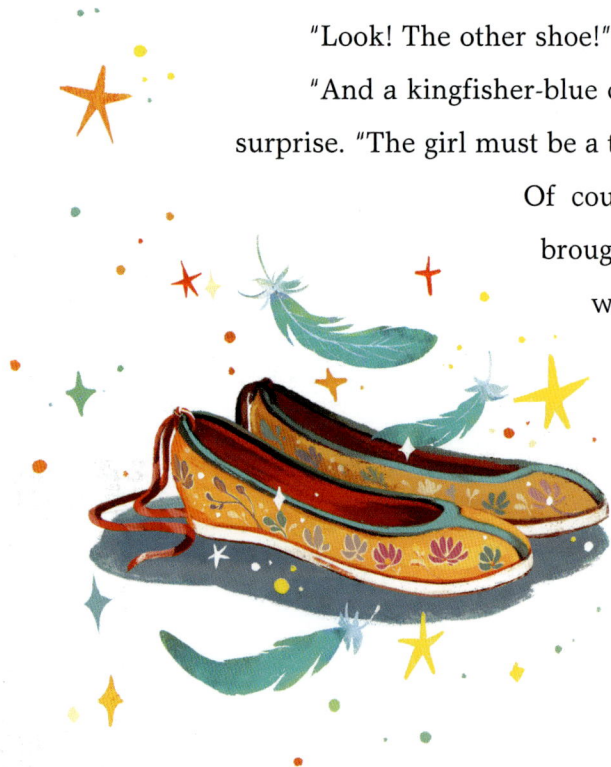

wishing bones back to his island kingdom. He wished for gold, jewels, pearls, fine clothes, bigger palaces and an unbeatable army... until one day the magic bones stopped granting wishes.

"These bones are useless now, throw them into the sea!" ordered the King.

But Ye-Tsien didn't throw them away. Carefully, she buried the wishing bones in the fine yellow sand of the beach, as if she were putting her best friend to bed, and whispered, "I wish I were far away from here."

And on the surface of the sea, there was a shimmering and a glittering...

The Stonecutter
A tale inspired by Japan

Having wishes granted is a special kind of magic. What would you wish for? This famous story of a poor stonecutter whose wishes come true has an interesting tale of its own! It happens among the mountains and pine forests of Japan but was probably written by a European writer who travelled to Japan and fell in love with its wondrous landscapes, buildings, customs – and, of course, stories.

Long ago, on a mountainside where white clouds meet green pine trees, there lived a poor stonecutter. Every day he chiselled out heavy blocks for roads, gravestones, statues and anything else people might need stone for. It was hard work, but the Stonecutter was happy.

One morning, the Stonecutter delivered a cartload of stones to a rich man in the nearby town. The Rich Man's house was grand, with servants running here and there, and a table loaded with delicious things to eat and drink.

"Leave the stones in the courtyard – my servants will collect them later," said the Rich Man.

The Stonecutter left, but along the road home he started thinking, *Why has the Rich Man got so much, and I so little?* And then he said out loud, "I wish I could be a rich man, with all those things!" Of course, he didn't expect anyone to hear him but something did.

Deep inside the earth lived the Spirit of the Mountain. It heard the voice of the Stonecutter and, in a flash, his wish was granted.

"Oh!" The Stonecutter looked around – he was standing outside a large house, with servants running this way and that, and kitchens full of cooks preparing delicacies. "I like this!" said the Stonecutter, and for a few days, he was happy.

One day, word came that the Emperor would be passing by the nearby town. Crowds lined the roads and cheered as the Emperor's golden palanquin passed by, followed by guards riding the finest horses. Everyone bowed to the Emperor but the Stonecutter thought again: *I'm a rich man now, but still I must bow to the Emperor,* and then he said out loud, "I wish I was a king with a palace, a throne, and gold and jewels in abundance!"

The Spirit of the Mountain heard and, in a flash, the Stonecutter was dressed in the heavy woven robes of an emperor, with armoured guards around him and a palace finer than the Stonecutter had ever imagined.

Ah! What riches! Now, I will surely be happy, he thought. And he was, all through spring until the summer, when he was sitting out in his palace gardens. The Sun beat down so hot and so fierce that he had to go inside.

"Huh! The Sun has forced me to act against my will – it is more powerful than any person. What good are riches without true power? I wish I was the Sun!" said the Stonecutter.

The Mountain heard and, in a flash, the Stonecutter became the Sun.

Wonderful! he thought, as he shone down hot and fierce, melting snow, drying crops and forcing people to take shelter inside. But then one day, a cloud passed over the Sun and stopped its heat from reaching the Earth.

"There IS something more powerful than the Sun. I wish I was a mighty cloud!" he said.

The Mountain heard and, in a flash, the Stonecutter became a cloud. The Stonecutter blocked the Sun and the Moon's light from Earth, shrouded mountains in mist, poured rain down on the land and the sea. But one day, the Wind blew the Cloud aside.

So the Stonecutter wished to become the Wind. He blew energy into windmills, blew the Sea into tsunamis and blew the coats off people's backs. But there was one thing that remained unmoved. The Mountain.

The Stonecutter wished and instantly he was a vast mountain, unchanging in the Sun, Rain or Wind. But what was that? Far down, past the clouds and the green pine trees at the base of the Mountain, there was a tiny figure. A Stonecutter, chiselling stone blocks from the mountainside.

"Little by little, that man can move mountains!" exclaimed the Stonecutter. Before he spoke another word, he became a Stonecutter once again, and lived so happily that he never made another wish.

Tom Tit Tot

A tale from England

Names carry a kind of magic all of their own. In many stories of enchantment and mystery, correctly guessing someone's true name can give you power over them, or even break a powerful enchantment. But what if the name is so unusual it's impossible to guess? In this English tale, full of strange gifts, mischief and surprise, name-guessing is a game – quite a dangerous one!

Once there was a daughter who was always hungry. And because she was always hungry, she could never think of anything but eating. And because she could never think of anything but eating, she never learned how to do anything else. One day, her mother baked five pies and left them on the windowsill to cool, but as soon as she wasn't looking, Daughter ate them all up.

At suppertime, Mother said, "Daughter, bring me one of those pies!"

"They're not cool enough yet!" lied the Daughter.

"Well, ready or not, here I come!" said Mother. But all that was left were

five empty dishes. "Daughter, you ate five pies today?"

"Yes, Mother, I did," Daughter said, wiping a pie crumb from her mouth.

Bother! Hungry, Mother sat down at her spindle, and began spinning flax into skeins of thread, chanting to the rhythm of the wheel: "Daughter ate five whole pies today! Daughter ate five whole pies today! Daughter ate five whole—"

"Five *WHAT*?" said a regal voice from outside the window.

The King was riding by. He was a very thin king who hated pies, and eating for that matter, but he loved newly spun thread.

"Oh! Your Majesty! I meant, Daughter has spun five *SKEINS* today!" Mother lied, flustered.

"Five WHOLE SKEINS! In five different weights? In five different colours?"

"Yes, of course!" she said nervously.

"A miracle!" shouted the King. "I will take your daughter to my palace immediately to be my queen. For eleven months she shall eat, wear and do what she wants. But in the twelfth month, she will spin five such skeins each day, or the bargain is broken and off with her head!"

So that day, Daughter became Queen. For eleven months she feasted on as much food as she could eat. On the morning of the twelfth month, the King led her to a tall room with a high window, filled with flax.

"As agreed, here is the flax for you to spin into fine thread. Five skeins each day, or off with your head!"

The door slammed shut and locked. Daughter, who had no idea how to spin or dye, began to cry. All day long she cried, so loudly that she didn't notice the scratching in the corner. Nor did she notice a tiny door open and a small

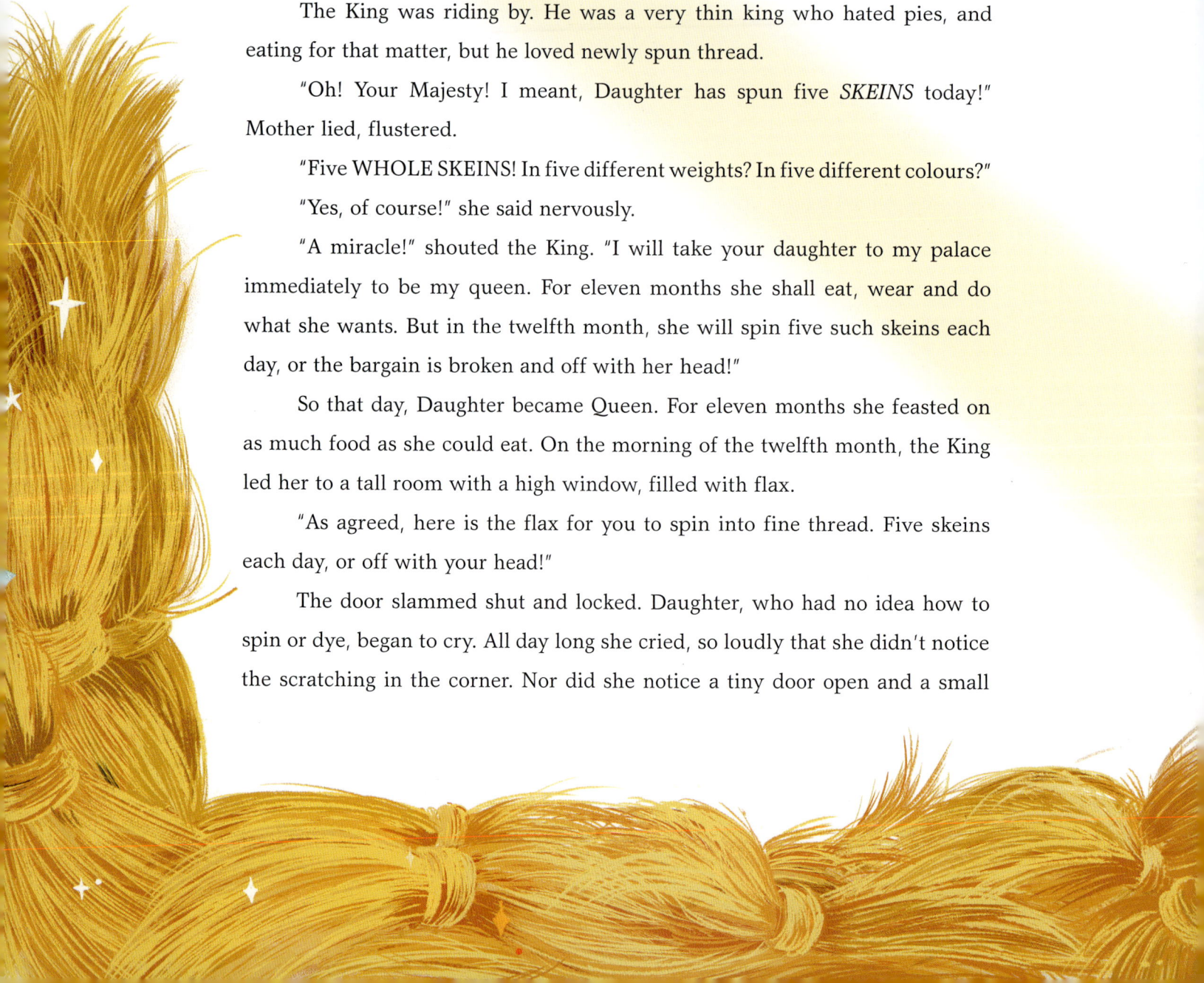

black shadow cross the room and wait at her feet. But then a voice spoke.

"Why do you weep?" said a small, pointy-tailed imp, looking up at her.

"Who are you? And what's it to you anyway?" Daughter sobbed.

"Never you mind who I am. This is about YOU. Perhaps I can help."

Then, because sharing is better than silence, the Daughter told the Imp everything.

"Ha ha ha! Now I see!" said the Imp. "Why don't you give the job to me? I'll take the flax and weave beautiful skeins of colour fit for a king!"

"But why would you do such a thing for me?"

The Imp danced and laughed. "Ha! You don't know me, it's all part of a game, you see! You must try to guess my name – for each five skeins, three guesses. If by the month's end you fail, you'll be mine and I'll take you to... WHO KNOWS WHERE!"

Thirty days in a month, three guesses a night – that's a lot of guesses! Surely, I'll guess right, thought Daughter. "Deal!" she told the Imp, who took the flax and disappeared through the door.

Daughter woke early the next morning and – THERE! – light streamed through the high window onto five skeins of thread – in five different colours and in five different weights!

"Beautiful!" said the King, when he looked in on her. "But remember, five more skeins tomorrow..."

That evening in the tall room, once again the tiny door opened and the pointy-tailed shadow darted across the floor.

"I spun, I dyed, I brought the skeins – now it's your turn: guess my name!"

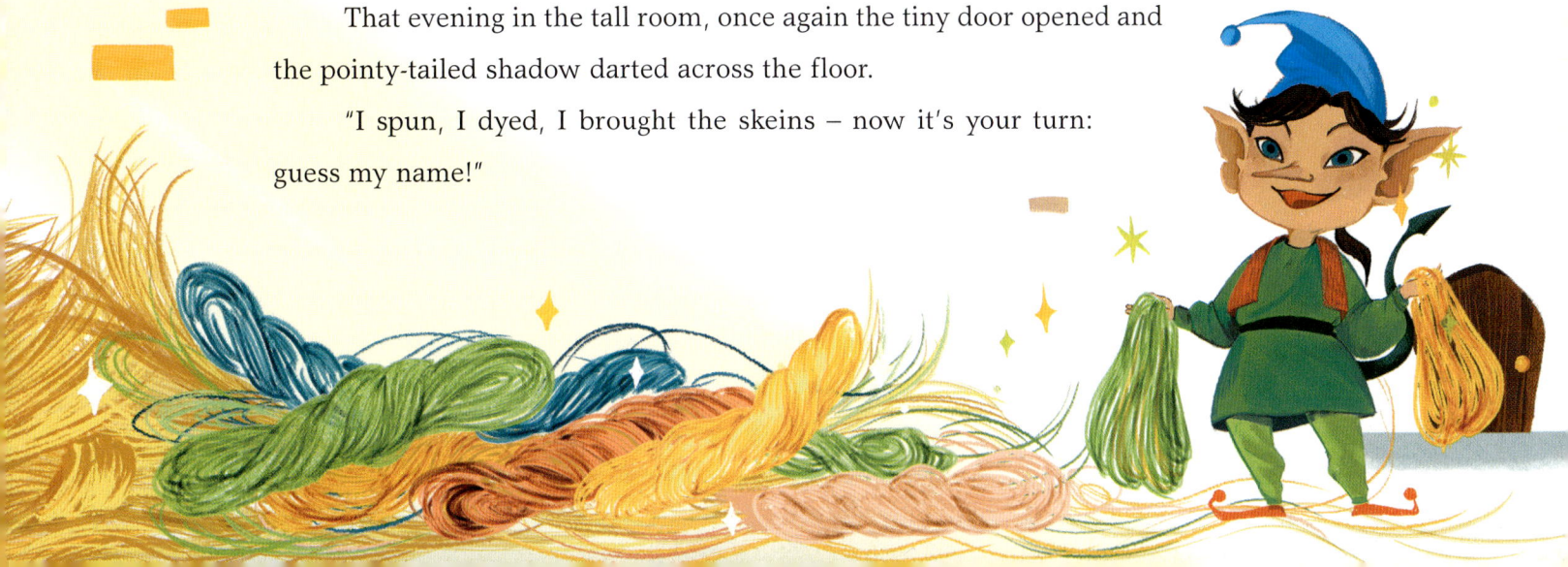

"Is your name Ben? Sam? Mark?"

"No! No! Nope!" cried the Imp. "I'll spin five more skeins and tomorrow we will play again!"

Every day that followed, there were five more skeins in five more colours for the King to collect. And each night, Daughter tried to guess the Imp's name. But the answer was always, "No, no. NOPE."

By day, Daughter read old books full of names. On the twenty-ninth day, she read the oldest book in the world, so she asked the Imp: "Is your name Enkidu? Ereshkigal? Gilgamesh?"

"NO! NO! NOPE!" The Imp danced and laughed. "Ha ha! One more day of wrong guesses and you'll be mine!"

The next morning, the King collected the skeins. "Wonderful work!" he said with delight. "One more day, and we'll be done. I'll have the world's finest clothes and you need never spin a skein again. Let's start celebrating now!"

He sat down and called for a feast to be brought. But then he began to laugh, louder and louder, until he shook.

"Why do you laugh?" asked Daughter.

"Well, this morning the strangest thing happened! I rode past a deep chalk pit and something caught my eye. A pointy-tailed shadow was spinning thread and singing a rhyme, which got stuck in my head:

Kettle and pot,
nose and snot,
she'll guess not,
I'm Tom Tit Tot!

The Daughter laughed, too, but said no more. Smiling to herself, she feasted well with the King.

That evening, the Imp arrived and sang, "Ha ha ha! The final game! Guess my name, guess my name!" So Daughter made her last three guesses.

"Is your name Ptah?"

"NO!"

"Sekhmet?"

"NO!"

"Is it TOM TIT TOT?"

"WHAT!?" the Imp asked, flabbergasted. "How did you guess my name?"

"How, indeed! I'll never tell!" Daughter replied.

If there's one thing imps hate, it's losing. With that the Imp sang a final rhyme:

I lost one, and you won one.
Let's play another game, resume the fun!
Come with me! Eat, laugh and play.
Better than this place any day!

Daughter had a choice. She made it. What she chose, and how she lived, is another story.

Oh, Tsar of the Forest
A tale from Ukraine

If you could change yourself into different animals or objects, what would you change yourself into? This story, which ranges across the wide grasslands and forests of Ukraine into underground worlds and back again, is about someone who learns shape-shifting magic because he is so bad at everything else. It is also about the very unusual kind of person who teaches him that magic, and what both master and apprentice choose to do with their powers.

Long ago, a father had a grown-up son so lazy that nobody in their town would take him as an apprentice. So, Father and Son were forced to travel further afield to find the Son work in the neighbouring kingdom. Their way took them across the great green valley and through a dark forest, until they came to a clearing full of tree stumps. The Father sat down and sighed, "Oh! I am so tired!"

Leaves rustled in the shadows. A small green hand emerged from a bush, belonging to a man who was green from his toes to his beard.

44

"Greetings. I am Oh, Tsar of the Forest. You called?" he said, imperiously. A tsar is like a king or emperor and they think of themselves as very important.

Astonished, Father just stared. So the strange green man continued.

"You said, 'Oh.' I am Oh. Why are you in my forest?"

"I seek a master, for my son to work for," Father replied.

"Oh," said Oh, "then I'll take him. He will learn what I teach him. Go — return in a year. If you recognise your son, you can take him back."

Father agreed without even asking what the job was and hurried home, leaving his son alone with Oh.

Oh clapped his hands, and he and the Son passed beneath the earth, until they came to an underground world where everything was green. In Oh's green cottage, the Son ate green food, drank green drink and, that night, slept in a green bed.

After a year, Father returned to the forest, and Oh took him down to his green cottage, where a flock of pigeons pecked and flapped in the yard.

"I teach the arts of transformation," he said. "Your son is one of those pigeons. Identify which one, and you may take him. If not, he stays with me!"

"All look busy except that lazy creature," replied Father, pointing to the one pigeon high up on the tree. "It's him!"

"Right you are!" scowled Oh. The pigeon instantly transformed back into the Son, fell off his perch and landed with a thump. The Tsar sighed. Father rolled his eyes, and went on his way with Son trotting behind.

As they walked along, Son said, "My master taught me the magic arts.

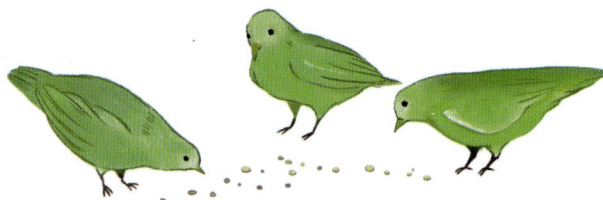

Now I can change into anything in the world!"

"That's not a real job," said Father. "Without money, we'll starve!"

"I can make money easily." The Son pointed to some hunters chasing a fox across green fields. "I'll become a greyhound and catch the fox. They'll want to buy me, and you must sell me without a collar for 300 silver pieces. Later, I'll change back, and we'll keep the money!"

Exactly as the Son said, the hunters bought the greyhound without the collar. But as soon as the hunt was done, the greyhound transformed back into the Son and ran back to his father, laughing. They continued on, until they came to a great marketplace.

"Here is where we'll make our real fortunes, Father!" declared the Son. "I'll become a horse, worth ten times a greyhound! Sell me without the bridle, and I will return as before."

The Son became a magnificent bay stallion, whose hooves struck sparks from the ground. Soon buyers crowded around. One – a tall, solemn figure in unfamiliar clothing – offered 3,000 silver coins, the best price by far, but insisted he must have the bridle, too. The price was so good that the Father agreed. He watched the buyer take the horse and bridle, then waited for his son as usual. But the Son did not return. Because this time, the buyer – none other than Oh, the Tsar of the Forest – had the bridle, so the horse could not escape.

Oh led the horse to a nearby lake to drink. But as soon as its lips touched the water, the horse became a stripy green perch and swam away. Instantly Oh transformed into a sharp-toothed pike and chased the perch across the lake but could not catch it.

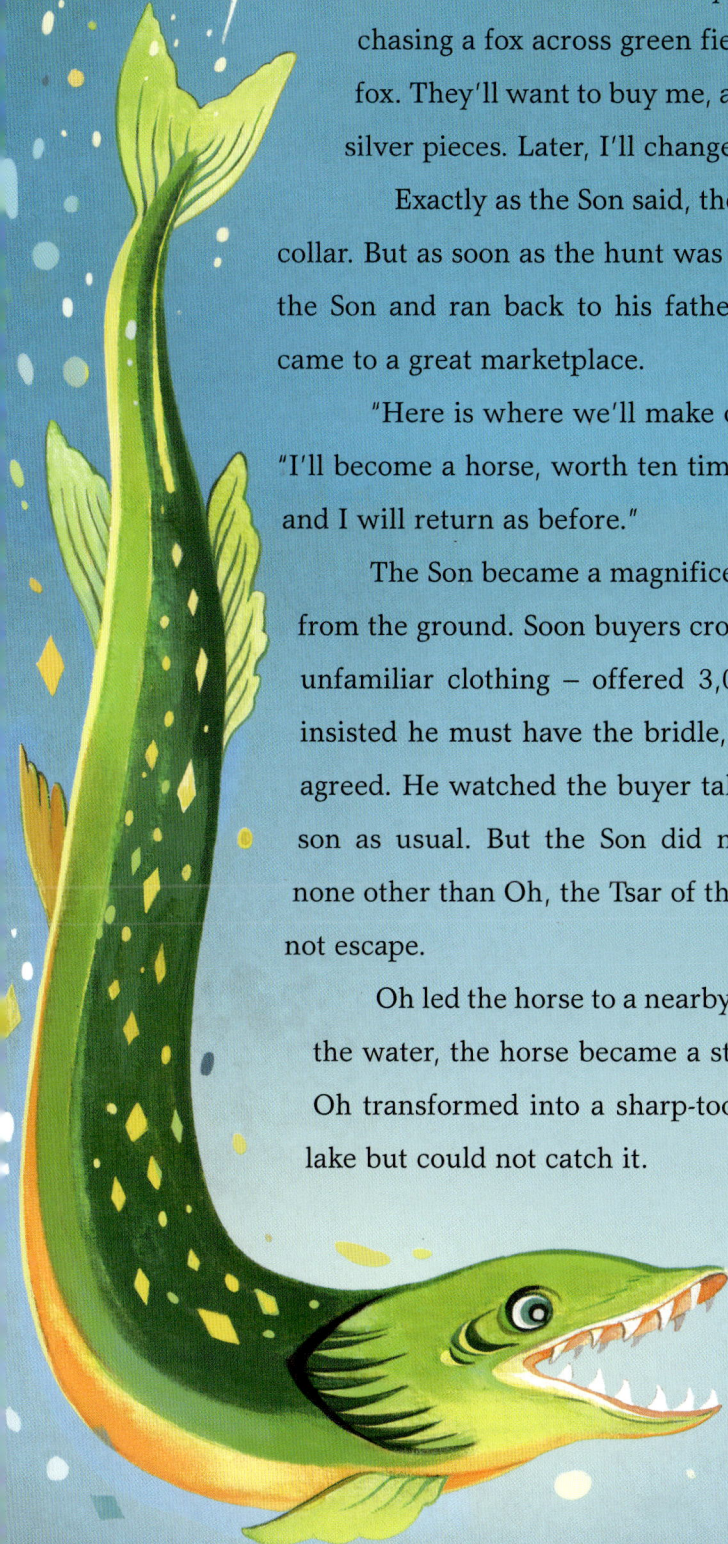

By the shore, a young woman was swimming when she saw a golden ring set with red garnets sparkling in the shallow water. The stripy green perch had changed into a ring!

"Beautiful!" the Young Woman gasped. She picked up the ring, put it on and returned to the market where she ran a stall with her mother. No sooner had she got there than she heard a wailing voice: "My ring! A reward to anyone who finds my ring!"

A Rich Man dressed in an expensive green coat stopped her and pointed at her finger. "Pardon me but is that ring yours? It looks just like the one I'm looking for. Give it to me!" he demanded.

His eyes suddenly glittered green, which seemed strange to the Young Woman. So instead of handing the ring over, she fumbled and dropped it in the dust, where it immediately became a pile of grain. Instantly the Rich Man became a rooster, pecked up the grains and flew away. But he had missed one grain that had rolled under the Young Woman's foot, which, when she moved it, became the Son again! The Father, still waiting, ran over and embraced him.

The Young Woman and her mother looked on in shock. "Who are you?" they asked. The Son told them and the two families ate together that night. The next day, they started a new business and the Son never had to change his shape again (unless he wanted to).

The Dove Princess
A tale from Poland

In this Polish tale, a brave princess sets out on an impossible journey she'll need magic to complete. The kingdom has fallen into ruin. Her father, the King, is so sad he cannot smile. Her stepmother – a cruel queen – has transformed her into a dove, and her twelve brothers into twelve golden eagles. But the little dove princess will not be defeated...

The little pale dove flew across fallow fields, wide lakes and mighty rivers.

I will never match an eagle's glide, I will never catch up! she thought, as she landed in the branches of a willow tree and began to coo with grief – for her father lost in sadness, for her brothers flying the wide world, and for herself.

But in the midst of her sorrow, she heard a voice from below, "Little Dove, do not lose hope!"

An old man with a white beard beckoned to her, and she flew down to him. With a willow wand he touched her lightly on the wing... and she was a girl again. Then he pressed a small loaf of bread into one of her hands, and a glass bottle into the other, and with a smile he slowly vanished, leaving an echo of a song in the Princess's heart:

Without shrinking this loaf will sustain you,
And this bottle will catch your tears.
Travel west towards the red sunset.
Sprinkle tears to heal sadness and fear.

The Princess travelled west, stopping only to rest when she was tired, or to eat from the everlasting loaf when she was hungry. The grasses sent whispers of courage to her ears, and she journeyed on for a year and a day. Until at last she reached the end of the world, where there was a wall and in the wall there was a closed door. The Princess knocked, and the door spoke!

"I am the door to the Ancestral Lands: those who pass through me never return!"

"I've searched the world for my eagle brothers," the Princess replied. "If they've crossed through then I must, too!"

"Eagles?! Twelve eagles?" the door exclaimed. "Every day they come, tired of this world, begging to pass – but I am locked to them, as I am to you, girl! And every day they fly away. But how will you leave this place, with no wings?"

The Princess looked up – and the world tipped on its side. The whole distance she had walked, from east to west, was now a vertical ravine of craggy rock, and the world she had left behind a pinprick of light up above her, far away.

"Not even an eagle could fly that far!" she said. "We are lost!"

Big, wet tears fell from her eyes and into the little bottle that the old man

had given her. When it was almost
full, the Princess felt a breeze on her
face, heard the beating of huge wings and
looked up again: twelve golden eagles swooped
down! They thrashed their wings against the door, and
their sad cries echoed around, but the door stayed shut. As they
turned to fly away, they saw the girl looking at them.

"Brothers, is that you?" she whispered.

Instantly, the eagles surrounded her. Now she knew what to do: taking
out the bottle, she sprinkled them with tears – and each eagle returned to his
human form. They all laughed and embraced each other, and the Princess
shared the everlasting loaf with them.

At the sounds of joy in that dark place, a beam of sunlight shone straight
down, and on it came the Bird of Paradise – 100 times the size of an eagle – with
her rainbow feathers, her beak and claws sparkling like ice in the sun, and her
kind eyes that gazed upon the Princess.

"Bird of Paradise! Please take us back to the light," the Princess implored,
and the bird bowed its head.

"Climb onto my back, and together we will return to the daylight land,"
she said. "But be warned – the journey is long, and I must be fed or I will fall,
and so will you…"

"I have bread!" said the Princess. "Brothers, climb up behind me!"

The great Bird of Paradise then flew up, carrying them all. The sun set, and rose again, and whenever the bird looked round, the Princess fed her from the loaf.

Another day passed, and on the third day, just as they were close to the top of the ravine with the blue sky above, the bird looked round. Before the Princess could feed her, the wind grabbed the loaf in its cold fingers and tossed it down into the ravine. Without food, the bird weakened, stopped rising and looked back in search of food again.

We have come too far to go back now! thought the Princess, and silently cut off one of her own fingers and gave it to the bird, who soared up again, strong and fast, until once more she looked round, and the Princess fed her another of her fingers. Then, at last, the bird and her passengers reached the top of the ravine.

"After the bread was lost, what did you feed me?" asked the bird.

When the Princess told her, the bird quickly breathed its Paradise breath onto the girl's wounded hand, and the Princess's fingers grew back as new.

"Farewell!" said the bird, and flew straight up into the blue sky.

As for the Princess and her brothers, they journeyed on until they reached home, not stopping to rest until the ruined kingdom was repaired, and the evil Queen had been defeated.

The King, who had been sad for many long years, smiled again when he saw them, and they all lived happily together.

The Foolish Brothers
A tale from India

It's easy to get carried away showing off our skills to impress others, without thinking about the consequences. This humorous story, about brothers competing with feats of magic, is one of many "teaching stories" from India, which demonstrate how we should (or shouldn't) behave!

Long ago, in a little house on the edge of the jungles of Madhya Pradesh, there lived four brothers, who loved competing with each other.

The day came for the elder brothers to go away to study at school. Three of them departed for different corners of the world. The fourth – the youngest – stayed at home, chasing small animals, talking to people and wondering what his brothers were learning so far away.

The years passed. In the jungle, tiny cinnamon shoots had grown up into fragrant trees, tall enough to shade a grown man. Then the three brothers – now grown men themselves – returned from their studies. The youngest brother met them on the road home and, as though they had never been apart, they immediately started competing as they went.

"Oh, you'll never guess the wonderful things *I'VE* learned to do!" boasted the eldest brother.

"I bet it's not as good as what *I* can do," bragged the second.

"Ha! That's nothing compared to *MY* successes!" crowed the third.

As they walked, the youngest listened to his brothers' voices, and the voices of the myna birds that flew overhead. Before long they came to a clearing covered by spreading tree branches that cast strange shadows. In the middle was a pile of huge white bones.

The eldest brother turned to the others. "Guess what?" he said. "When I was away, I studied the arts of architecture and construction, and I was the best student. If I wanted, I could recreate a whole skeleton from just one bone!"

"No! Impossible!" his brothers said, shaking their heads.

"I'll prove it!" said the eldest brother. He picked up the largest bone and began to chant and wave his arms in complicated patterns. The air hummed and the bone quivered... Then it grew another bone. And then another and another. Until, shining in the dim light, was the complete skeleton of a King Tiger!

"Very clever!" said the second brother. "But not as clever as what I learned while I was away. I studied biotechnology and healing. I can make organs, muscles, skin and fur to fill and cover this skeleton!"

Standing before the skeleton, as the eldest had done, the second brother chanted and waved his arms. There was a hum in the air, then an invisible wave of force, and then – *POP!* – organs appeared, muscles stretched themselves to

and fro, and a striped blanket of fur wrapped itself neatly around it all. The brothers gaped. There, in the moonlight, lay the huge body of a King Tiger.

"YOU might think that's good," said the third brother, "but what I learned beats all of that! Because I learned true magic! I can breathe life into any body!" He took a deep breath—

"STOP!" said the youngest brother, climbing a tall tree for safety. "This is a jungle, that is a King Tiger! It would be foolish to bring it to life."

"Why are you scared? He's lying!" the second brother told the youngest.

"Yeah, he'll never be able to do it," smirked the eldest brother.

"Just watch me!" the third brother said.

The others looked on as he chanted and waved his hands. Unknown magic unfurled from his fingers into the air and settled slowly on the huge cat. The creature opened its eyes, looked around and stood up. Then, the brothers heard a rumble, worse than the sound of thunder. The King Tiger remembered it had not eaten in a long time as it met the gaze of the brothers. It crouched and its eyes gleamed, casting a huge tiger shadow on the dark ground.

The three eldest brothers, who had learned a lot of magic but not much sense, ran away as fast as they could. The youngest brother, who had learned no magic but saw sense first, tried to distract the King Tiger with noise from the safety of the tree. He could only watch on helplessly as it set off through the jungle after his three brothers.

Perhaps the tiger caught up with the brothers and ate them for its breakfast. Perhaps they escaped or perhaps they are still running...

The Star Husbands

A tale from North America

Variations of this tale exist in indigenous communities on the North American continent, including the Mi'kmaq people, whose territory now lies in Southeastern Canada. Some say the star husbands in the story are inspired by Sirius, our brightest and closest star, also known as the "Dog Star", which appears in the Canis Major constellation, and Betelgeuse, a bright "red" star in the constellation of Orion. Wolverine is a famous trickster figure of great power and mischief, who features in many stories from the region, as Coyote and Raven do further south.

Long ago, in a country of clear skies and cold waters, there lived two sisters known as "weasel" for their silky hair and fast footsteps. Their husbands – two brothers – were always fighting. One day, Eldest said to Youngest, "Enough! Let's leave here!"

Along a path, through a forest and along a valley, the sisters went as fast as they could. At sunset, they stopped and made camp in a clearing by a fast-

flowing creek under tall spreading white pine trees. They cooked and ate, then lay down. But before they slept, they looked up at the vast, sparkling night sky.

Youngest pointed up. "Look, sister! Stars are better than men. I wish a star could be my husband! I'd choose that big bright white one, there!"

Eldest looked up, too. "I'd choose that smaller, fiery-red star – that's the one for me!"

Both sisters laughed as they lay under their furs, and it wasn't long before they slept. Sleep so deep that they did not notice their wishes had been granted until they woke at first light in an unfamiliar tent, in an unfamiliar camp, and knew in their hearts they were not on Earth anymore, but in Star Country. Youngest rolled over and looked around.

"Wife! Don't spoil my preparations!" a voice barked.

It was the voice of the White Star, in the form of a great hunter, shining brightly enough to dazzle her eyes and almost stop her breath.

Eldest rolled over and looked round.

"Stop FIDGETING, wife!" a second voice barked. It was the Red Star, whose grumpy old eyes blinked fast like flickering candles.

"Wives, we will go and hunt now," the Red Star and the White Star told them gruffly. "Stay here and work. Whatever you do, do not lift the White Stone." And then the Star Husbands were gone.

Outside the tent, Star Country was old and wild, with rocks everywhere but no forests or river valleys. There was work, but the sisters didn't know how to braid star-rope or weave star-baskets, and nobody was there to teach them. Their Star Husbands were strange, and did not return that night or the next.

One morning, despite the Star Husbands' instruction not to, the sisters lifted the White Stone and under it saw the world they'd left behind, far below. Regretful and sad, the sisters' tears fell down through the hole and were swallowed up by the atmosphere below.

With each day, the sisters became more homesick. They even tried making a rope ladder to take them back down to Earth, but it wasn't long enough.

"I wish we'd never come here," the sisters cried.

The Star Husbands knew everything. They knew that the sisters had looked under the White Stone, and they knew that the sisters longed for home.

Because this was Star Country, and stars see all.

"We should let them return to their own land," the flickering Red Star told the big White Star, who agreed.

The Star Husbands then crossed the star plains and greeted the sisters with soft voices, so that they would not be afraid.

"Tonight, sleep under the furs you brought with

you," said the White Star. "But in the morning, when you hear the chickadee sing, close your eyes and do not come out."

"Then the red squirrel will cry – but wait," added Red Star. "When you hear the striped squirrel – THAT is when you must emerge. You will be home and Star Country will be as far away as it ever was."

The sisters understood and fell asleep smiling. In the morning, Youngest heard the red squirrel's cry, but mistook it for the striped squirrel. She jumped out from under the furs and looked down. And down. She and Eldest were perched on a tiny nest, at the top of a tall white pine tree!

"We have come out too early! How will we get down?" she said to Eldest.

Far, far below, they saw two familiar figures walk by.

"Husbands – it is us!" shouted Eldest, but they walked on and did not hear. Then Bear came along.

"Help us down and we will repay you!" both sisters shouted.

But Bear walked on, too. Then Pine Marten appeared, but he walked by also.

Last of all came Wolverine, sauntering alone, whistling a tune. He looked up and he saw two beautiful sisters, pale and quick as weasels. He saw a fine opportunity.

"Ladies! Sisters! It seems you need assistance to descend from this tree: if I help, what will you give me?'

The sisters were young, but they knew Wolverine; everyone did. Always trying tricks – hungry for mischief!

"He wants to kidnap us and marry us!" whispered Eldest.

"But we need to get down," hissed Youngest.

The sisters quickly hatched a plan. They removed Youngest's hair ribbons and tangled them in the uppermost branches of the tall white pine tree.

"Wolverine!" they called out. "Bring us down and treat us well, and we'll decorate your tent with beauty!"

A fine bargain! thought Wolverine so he climbed up and then brought the sisters down, one by one.

At the bottom of the white pine tree, Youngest gasped, "Oh dear! My hair ribbon. I've left it in the tree! I can't build anything without it. Please, Wolverine, go up and bring it down, untangled in one piece. A broken ribbon is a curse. While you work, we will decorate your tent with beauty!"

Wolverine climbed back up, but untangling the ribbon took a very long time. When he finally returned, his tent was indeed decorated – but with sharp thorns and stinging hornets, which pierced and stung him all over.

And the sisters – known as "weasels" for their silky hair and their fast footsteps – were long gone!

Snow White
A tale from Germany

This well-loved wonder tale of evil plots, magic mirrors and strong emotion, was being told out loud in Germany long before it was ever written down. But it only became famous across the world after German story-collectors the Brothers Grimm published it in writing. The story is rich and strange, full of contrasting colours, secret spells and stark images, which help bring it to life in your imagination.

Once there was a queen who loved beautiful things; her own beauty most of all. She owned a magic mirror and every morning she asked of it:

> *Mirror, mirror, on my wall*
> *Who in this land is fairest of all?*

The mirror could not lie, and it always gave the same answer:

> *You, Oh Queen, are fairest of all.*

One winter's day, the Queen sat sewing at an open window, watching snow fall on the ebony windowsill.

"Ouch!" She pricked her finger, and three red drops of blood fell onto the white snow on the black sill.

Beautiful colours... I wish I had a child just as beautiful! she thought, and her wish was granted: a daughter black as ebony, red as blood and white as snow. She was named Snow White, and each day she grew more beautiful. Until one day, the mirror that could not lie answered the Queen:

You, Queen, are of the fairest few,
But Little Snow White is fairer than you.

The Queen's jealousy grew and twisted her heart until she decided that Snow White must die. She commanded a hunter to take the girl on a three-day journey into the deep woods, kill her and return to her with proof. The Hunter obeyed, but when it came to it, he could not bring himself to kill the girl.

"Run!" he said, and instead he killed a boar, bringing its lungs and liver back to the Queen, proclaiming that they were Snow White's. Satisfied, the Queen asked the mirror:

Who in this land is fairest of all?

This time, the mirror answered:

Though you, Queen, are of the fairest few,
In the seven mountains, where miners dig jewels,
Snow White still lives, and is fairer than you.

The Queen was furious. "That Hunter tricked me, and the dwarf miners of the seven mountains have rescued her!"

Envy wrung her heart without rest, until she hit upon another way to kill Snow White. Disguised as an old peddler woman, the Queen left the castle, and journeyed through the woods towards the seven mountains.

Snow White was indeed alive and safe with the dwarf miners. On that terrible day, they had found her asleep in their cottage having run a long way over sharp stones. When she awoke and told them her story, they took pity and invited her to stay and tend the house while they worked.

One afternoon, alone at the cottage, Snow White heard a voice: "Pretty things for sale!" it sang. From the window, she saw an old woman holding a laced ribbon woven from silk of red, yellow and blue.

"A lace for your bodice, pretty as you!" she called, and so Snow White opened the door for a closer look. "I'll lace you in!" the old woman said, grasping the bodice and lacing it so tight that Snow White could hardly breathe and fell down as if dead. The Queen hurried back to ask the magic mirror:

Who in this land is fairest of all?

But the mirror answered:

Though you, Queen, are of the fairest few,
Snow White still lives and is fairer than you!

"No! Snow White must die!" the Queen raged. She made a poisoned comb, disguised herself once again and set out into the deep dark woods.

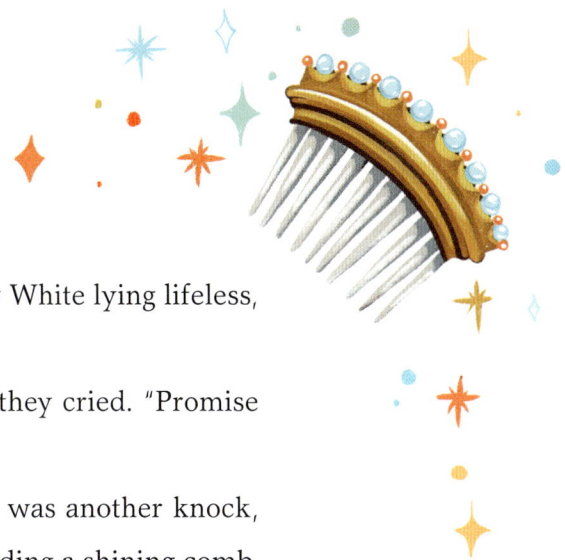

In the mountain cottage, the seven miners had found Snow White lying lifeless, but when they cut the too-tight laces, she breathed again.

"This is the work of someone who means you ill," they cried. "Promise not to open the door while we are out!"

Snow White promised. But the next afternoon there was another knock, another voice, another old woman outside the window, holding a shining comb.

"It won't hurt to look!" cajoled the old woman.

"The comb *is* pretty, and this old woman seems a harmless stranger," Snow White reasoned, and opened the door.

Instantly the old woman stuck the poisoned comb into Snow White's scalp, and again she collapsed, as though dead. The Queen then hurried home to the magic mirror. But to her horror, the answer was the same:

Though you, Queen, are of the fairest few,
Snow White still lives and is fairer than you!

"Curses!" Envy kicked and pinched the Queen until she vowed, "Snow White will die if it's the last thing I do!"

In a secret room, she took a beautiful apple – white one side, red on the other – and poisoned the red half. In another disguise, the Queen set off again.

Back at the cottage, Snow White's seven friends had found her, pulled out the poisoned comb, revived her, and made her promise to open the door to *nobody*.

But the next day, under the open window, another old woman held a basket of apples so delicious looking that Snow White longed to taste one.

"No need to open the door, take one as a gift," said the old woman, offering up an apple. "Don't fear and fuss! I'll split one with you."

The old woman cut the apple and, taking a bite of the white half, offered Snow White the red half. "Rosy, just like your cheeks!" she cooed.

Unable to resist, Snow White reached out, took a bite... and fell down dead.

"Let your seven friends try and wake you now!" cackled the Queen and hurried back to the magic mirror. Its answer calmed the envy in her heart at last:

You, Oh Queen, are fairest of all.

Later that evening, the seven miners found Snow White, but nothing could revive her, and for three days and nights they mourned. But Snow White's cheeks stayed warm and rosy, as if she were only asleep, and they could not bear to bury her. Instead, they made a magnificent glass coffin, inlaid with jewels from the seven mountains, with her name tooled in gold, so they could see her always. They placed her inside the coffin, carried it to the top of the seventh mountain, and kept watch day and night.

One day, a young prince rode by. When he saw Snow White in the glass coffin, he fell instantly in love and could go no further.

"Sell me this treasure!" he asked, but the seven miners refused. "Then give her to me freely. Of all the living things in this wide world, Snow White is the most precious to me," he pleaded.

The miners saw that the Prince spoke love's truth.

"Very well, but you must take good care of her," they said. But as they lifted the glass coffin, one stumbled. The sudden movement dislodged the poisoned piece of apple in Snow White's throat, and she opened her eyes. In wonder, she lifted the lid, and looked up at the overjoyed faces of her seven friends, and a royal prince. Joyfully, they ate together, and when the Prince confessed his love and asked her to marry him, she said yes.

Across the surrounding kingdoms everyone accepted invitations to the royal marriage. On the day of the wedding, the oblivious Queen stood before the mirror in her finest clothes:

Mirror, mirror, on my wall
Who in this land is fairest of all?

She was horrified when it answered:

Though you, Queen, are of the fairest few,
The bride, the young Queen, is fairer than you!

"My daughter? Alive? A Queen?!" she cried. Her envy – heavy, red-hot iron shoes – dragged her to the celebrations. When she recognised Snow White, the iron shoes made her dance... until she fell down dead.

The Bird of the Golden Feather
An Arabic tale

This story of treasures, peril and magical companions is based on tales collected in Iraq and Syria. It happens in a fantastical world where supernatural beings such as Djinn interact with humans, and where the smallest object can start the greatest adventure. It begins when a golden bird visits a royal palace garden and flies off leaving a magnificent feather. At the king's command, his three sons ride off in search of the bird – but only the two eldest princes return, with the terrible news that Kassim, the youngest, has been lost. The whole city mourns alongside the king...

In a tiny alleyway beside a grand bazaar in a city of joy and sorrow, there lived a goldsmith who owned a shop nobody ever visited. Then one day, his luck changed: he hired a new apprentice who was so cheerful and well-spoken that customers came from near and far. Word of the shop spread all the way to the royal palace. The Goldsmith was summoned by the King's sons – a great honour – but returned terrified, crying, "I have forty days to live!"

The Goldsmith held up three items: a silver pistachio containing a ring that reflected light just so, a woven-metal bracelet encased in a golden almond and a spider-silk dress folded inside a diamond hazelnut.

"This work is exquisite, not of this world, beyond even my skill. But the King's sons ordered me to make exact replicas within forty days, or I'll be executed!" he cried.

The Apprentice smiled. "Master, leave this to me," he said.

The Goldsmith was astounded. "Where...? How...? Wait. Who are you?"

"From further-than-far, another world," said the youth. "Sir, I am Kassim."

"The King's lost youngest son?!"

"Yes, he – who rode after the Bird of the Golden Feather. I have a story to tell, if you will listen." The Goldsmith nodded. Kassim began:

❖ ◈ ❖ ◈ ❖ ◈ ❖ ◈ ❖

My brothers and I rode fast on fine horses, and after forty days we reached a place where the road split into three. We each took a different path: mine wound steeply uphill to a mountaintop where I saw a huge figure, sitting still as a rock, covered in tangled hair. I knew instantly it was a mighty being from the land of the Djinn! I called out in awe, just as the Djinn looked down at me. Its voice was thunder, but its eyes were sad. "Oh! Young human, you are the first soul I have seen in a hundred years! Will you help me with my hair?"

I was honoured to help such a marvellous creation and I set to work immediately, washing and trimming. When I had finished, the Djinn was so happy it offered me a wish. All I wanted was to find the golden-feathered bird for my father, so I asked for its help.

At first the Djinn refused, saying "a mere human could never succeed in this task!" But I pleaded, begged and insisted, and at last the Djinn agreed. It scooped me up and carried me high over mountains and valleys to the gates of a magnificent palace garden. Then, it gave me these instructions: "This garden is full of exquisite birds of every kind, singing beautiful music. The Bird of the Golden Feather sleeps in a golden cage at the very end of the garden. Take only what you came for. TOUCH NOTHING ELSE!"

The Djinn could not pass the gates, so I walked alone through the garden until I reached the bird in its golden cage – what a marvel it was! As instructed, I picked it up and hurried back. But as I neared the gate, I heard a song so divine that I could not resist the urge to reach out for the bird that sang it. That was a mistake – instantly all the birds cried out, "STRANGER!"

Guards came running and marched me before the King of that palace.

"The penalty for stealing is death!" he cried.

I was terrified, but I tried to reason with him. "You'll kill me for the sake of a bird my father needs? I am a king's son, as you are a king. Please give the bird to me!"

To my surprise, he nodded: "Bring me the Fastest Horse in the World, and you may take the bird," he commanded.

I hurried back to the Djinn, who was angry with me for touching what I promised not to touch. But it could not be undone. I swore to follow the Djinn's instructions if it would carry me to the land of the Fastest Horse in the World, and soon we were at the stables of another magnificent palace.

The Djinn warned me, "Enter the stable, saddle the horse with a plain harness and lead it back here. TOUCH NOTHING ELSE!"

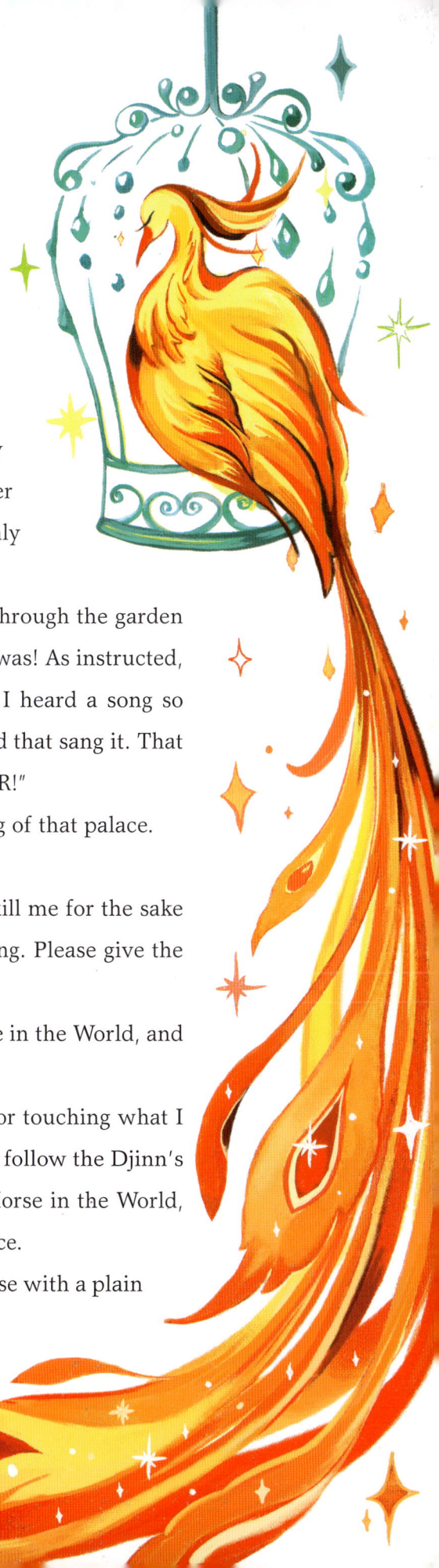

I obeyed, but as I led the horse back, I saw a glittering jewel sparkling on the ground, so beautiful I could not resist the urge to reach for it.

"STRANGER!" it cried. Again, guards marched me before the palace king, who threatened to execute me. Again, I tried to reason with him. At last, he agreed to give me the horse in exchange for a fruit from the Garden of Eternal Life.

The Djinn was waiting for me, enraged – but I needed its help more than ever. When I vowed in tears to TOUCH NOTHING BUT THE FRUIT, it flew me to the Garden of Eternal Life, grumbling all the way. There, I plucked one exquisite golden fruit from a tree so heavy with them I couldn't help reaching for just one more.

Once again, I was forced to plead for my life and return to my friend the Djinn for help, for the King's price for the fruit was the highest yet: Badia, the Unconquerable Princess of the Djinn.

The Djinn was furious: "Stupid boy! Princess Badia makes her own choices. She is fierce. Your life will be in her hands. Go to her. If her eyes are red, you may explain yourself, but I warn you: if they flash gold, run!"

The Djinn then flew me farther-than-far to its own land. At the royal palace, I presented myself to Princess Badia. She was magnificent – I loved her at first sight. When she saw me, her eyes remained red. I explained my quest and asked her to come with me. She agreed because she loved me, too!

"When you succeed, we will marry. Accept these betrothal gifts, beloved." Badia clapped her hands and three sparkling nuts fell from the air. "This silver pistachio contains a ring made of metal only found in this land. This golden almond contains a bracelet braided in a pattern known only here. And this diamond hazelnut contains a dress woven from spider-silk you will never see elsewhere. Only two of each exist. I have the others."

Together, we flew back to the Garden of Eternal Life, but, of course, I could not part with my love. So, we played a trick: the Djinn transformed into the shape of Badia, and before the King I exchanged "her" for the fruit. But the moment "she" was alone, the Djinn-in-disguise vanished from the palace and reappeared at our meeting place. With the fruit AND Badia, we flew to the land of the Fastest Horse in the World and played the same trick.

Then, with Badia and the fruit, on the Fastest Horse, we flew to the land of the Bird of the Golden Feather and did it again! The Djinn flew us back to the crossroads where my journey began, before returning to its mountain with my eternal thanks.

My brothers' paths were less lucky than mine – I found them living as paupers in a nearby city. I introduced them to my beloved, showed them the bird, the horse and the fruit, and we started for home together. They seemed overjoyed to see me – but they were plotting.

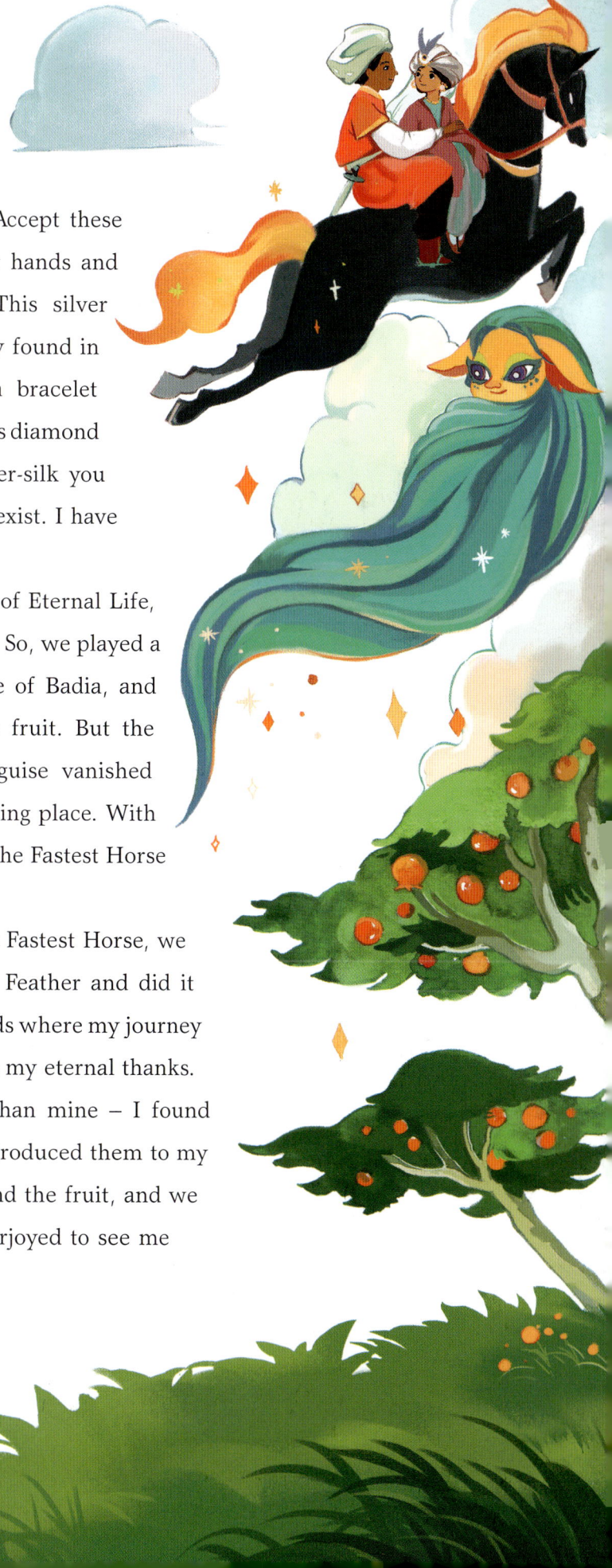

On the journey, they threw me down a well, left me for dead and rode back here, claiming Badia and everything else as theirs. But I escaped and, hidden in disguise as your apprentice, heard that the bird's golden feathers had turned white, the fruit had shrivelled and the horse could not run.

Badia was clever: she refused my brothers unless they could bring exact replicas of her gifts – impossible for anyone but me. When she sees them, she will know I am alive, and I can return.

And sure enough, when the Goldsmith presented the gifts at the palace, Badia told the King everything and the brothers were banished. Her eyes flashed gold with anger – but when she saw Kassim, her eyes turned red again.

"Son, you're alive!" The King kissed and embraced Kassim. The Bird of the Golden Feather became gold again and flew away but the King was so happy he did not care. Kassim and Badia were married – and on the Fastest Horse in the World, holding the Fruit of Eternal Life, they rode off into many other adventures together.

Blodeuwedd

A tale from Wales

This story is from the Mabinogion – a big patchwork of stories rooted in the green, mountainous landscape of Wales. From a mythical world full of magic and mystery, war and peace, love and hate – and actions that have serious consequences – the story of Blodeuwedd is not one of easy answers or happy endings. But, if you dare to venture into this powerful story, it has the power to enrich your heart and soul.

Long ago, at the court of the wizard-king Math, in the land of Gwynedd, the Lady Arianrhod cast three *tynged* spells on her son in a furious rage to punish her brother Gwydion:

> *You will have no name unless I name you,*
>
> *You will hold no weapons unless I arm you,*
>
> *You will marry no woman living now on this Earth.*

But over time, Gwydion, a powerful magician, broke his sister's spells one by one... By the time her son became a man, he had a name, Lleu Llaw Gyffes, and

he held his own sword. But to find him a wife, Gwydion needed help from King Math. Together they hatched a plan.

"If Lleu cannot take a wife of this Earth, then we will make him one," they decided. And on a grassy riverbank, they gathered oak flowers in green clusters, yellow sprays of broom and white clouds of meadowsweet. With these flowers they made a living woman, and named her Blodeuwedd – Flower-face – who was as beautiful as sunrise, and as fragrant as blossoms.

The moment golden-haired Lleu saw her, he loved her, and they were married. King Math gave them land and a castle at Mur Castell in the Ardudwy highlands, where Lleu ruled wisely.

One morning, Blodeuwedd stood alone, staring at the forest that separated the castle from the world outside. Lleu was away at King Math's court – again. Blodeuwedd sighed, then heard a strange noise in the distance. A hunting horn! A stag appeared, running, chased by men on horseback.

"Who leads this hunt?"she asked a passing manservant.

"Gronw Pebr, Lord of Penllyn, my lady," he replied.

"Lleu always shows hospitality; let us host this Lord tonight!" she said.

Gronw accepted the invitation, and when Blodeuwedd went to greet him he bowed in thanks. When he raised his head and saw her – as beautiful as sunrise – words left him. Their eyes met, and in an instant Blodeuwedd knew him in a way she had never known Lleu.

"Stay," she said, and so Gronw did. Together, they ate, drank, talked and laughed. After three days they were so deeply in love that they could not bear being apart. But they knew the only way they could be together was if Lleu Llaw Gyffes was dead.

When Lleu returned to the castle, Blodeuwedd seemed different. When he spoke to her, she did not reply.

Blodeuwedd

"What is wrong?" he asked.

"I am worried," she said. "What if you die before me?"

Lleu laughed. "Do not worry, I am hard to kill."

"Oh, really?" she replied, eyes wide.

"Yes. The only weapon that can kill me is a spear, made over a whole year, and only on Sundays when working is forbidden."

"Really?"

"Yes. And more, I cannot be killed by day or by night, clothed or naked, riding or walking, indoors or outdoors."

"So how *can* you be killed?"

"Only at twilight, between day and night, dressed in a net, which covers me but is not clothing. One foot must be on a billy goat's back, and the other on the side of a bathtub, all underneath a twig-roofed shelter with no walls. Only THEN can that spear kill me. Calm yourself, my dear, you have no need to worry!"

"A very exact combination." She nodded. "My mind is at rest!"

But Blodeuwedd 's mind was not at rest at all. It was busy. She sent word to Gronw Pebr to make a spear, every Sunday for a year, as Lleu had described. Finally, on the day after it was completed, Gronw hid on a hill above the river Cynfael as agreed, while Blodeuwedd spoke to Lleu.

"Husband, about what you said last year... I can't quite imagine it. Can you show me?"

Though Lleu was puzzled, he agreed. "Anything for you," he said.

And so the necessary elements came together. On the riverbank, as Lleu stood under the wooden shelter, in a net, with one foot on a billy goat's back and the other on a bathtub, Gronw stood and threw the spear down the hill.

Blodeuwedd

It flew through the air and pierced Lleu's side. He shrieked in shock, jumped and became an eagle, which flew away.

"At last, we can be together!" Gronw and Blodeuwedd rejoiced. They returned to Mur Castell, and lived in secret as husband and wife.

But King Math's ears could hear any secret. He told Lleu's uncle, Gwydion, who walked from green Gwynedd over mountains and marshes to find eagle Lleu. On his way, Gwydion stayed with a peasant who kept a pig that ran off every morning, but returned well fed. Puzzled, Gwydion followed it to a valley, where he saw scraps of meat falling from an oak tree. He looked up. In the treetop was an injured eagle. Gwydion knew it must be Lleu so sang him an *englyn* song:

> *Oh Oak, that lies between two lakes*
> *Silent, sheltering glen and sky.*
> *This fate is – Lleu, I do not lie –*
> *Flower-face's fault, that is why.*

He sang until the eagle-shaped Lleu flew down and Gwydion changed him back into a man. Then he went to hunt for Bloeuedd. She tried to run, flower-fragrance streaming behind her, but Gwydion was powerful, and she was his creation. By a lake shore, he overtook her and cast a spell:

> *I made you: I can unmake you! But instead, I will change you.*
> *From this day, Flower-face will be Owl.*
> *Birds will hate you, animals will fear you, and you will hide*
> *from the sun that nourished you!*

The words rang out – and an owl silently spread its wings and swooped away.

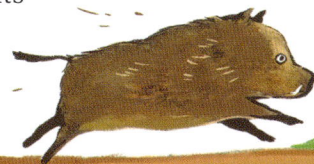

The Doll and the Light
A tale from Russia

In Russian and Eastern European stories, there's a character who doesn't just do magic, she is magic. Some say she is the greatest witch ever: her name is Baba Yaga. She is old but strong, and one of her legs is bare bone. She flies at night – not on a broomstick, but in a huge mortar and pestle. If she's hungry, she might eat you – but if you're brave and clever like Vasilisa, she might decide to help you instead...

Long, long ago, in a city not too far away from a dark, evergreen forest, a young girl called Vasilisa lived happily with her mother and father. Until Vasilisa was eight, when her mother fell ill and called Vasilisa to her bedside. Pressing a tiny doll into her hand, she said, "Daughter – this doll is my blessing to you. She is like no other. Always keep her with you, and when you need good advice, feed her a little: she will help you when I cannot."

When her mother died, Vasilisa's tears soaked the doll, whose little eyes and little mouth opened. She was alive!

"Sleep now, love," said the doll. "Sadness bites at night. The morning is wiser than the evening."

Vasilisa slept, and then woke. She felt a little better.

One day, her father came home with someone new.

"Daughter, greet your new mother. She will help you in ways I cannot," he said. Then he was gone.

New Mother's mouth smiled, but her eyes were cold. "This is my house now. Do as I say, and you can stay," she warned.

Days, months, years of hard work went by. Vasilisa grew into a strong, skilled young woman. She never complained, not even when New Mother moved them to a new house, half-swallowed by the great forest's edge, and made Vasilisa spin and weave from dawn to dark. Then one night, New Mother put out all the fires, and woke Vasilisa.

"The wind blew the fires out!" she lied. "Go into the forest and ask our closest neighbour for a light."

"Who?" Vasilisa asked, though she knew who. Everyone knew.

Baba Yaga! Nobody's daughter!
Flies around in a pestle and mortar!
Iron teeth, bony leg, fly-by-night, friend of death, and—

"I'm sure the rumours aren't true! She'd never eat a girl as bony as you!" laughed New Mother. "All vicious rumours! Now go!"

With her New Mother's cruel voice ringing in her ears, Vasilisa walked alone through the dark forest. It was cold and lonely, but the little doll was in her pocket to

keep her company. Dawn came, and with it a whisper from inside Vasilisa's pocket. "Listen!"

Vasilisa heard hoofbeats thundering closer – *whoosh!* A white horse, carrying a rider dressed all in white, galloped past.

"Follow!" said the doll. Vasilisa kept walking, and as day broke – *whoosh!* A red horse, carrying a red rider, roared past.

"Follow!" hissed the doll.

Vasilisa followed. All day, past sunset into the deepest, darkest part of the forest – *whoosh!* Black horse, black rider. "Follow!" said the doll a third time.

Vasilisa walked on until she came to a fence of white bones. From each fence post, a yellow light flickered from the eye sockets of a skull. Baba Yaga's fence! Behind the fence, on trees like giant chicken's legs, was a house, with a door that faced the forest. Baba Yaga's house!

The wind howled, the trees shook, and with a SNAP of teeth, a HISS of willow broom and a CRACK of stone, Baba Yaga landed.

"House! Face me, not the forest!" she commanded. The house obeyed. Baba Yaga stopped and took a long, deep sniff. "Human girl, show yourself!"

Vasilisa stepped out from the shadows.

"I am Vasilisa. New Mother sent me to borrow a light, to start our fires."

"Oh, did she now? Well, you don't get something for nothing," said Baba Yaga. "Come into my house, work for me, and if you do well you will have what you want. If you don't – well, then, I'm sure you've heard the rumours – there is ALWAYS space inside my belly. So, do your best!"

The bone gate in the bone fence swung inwards, the

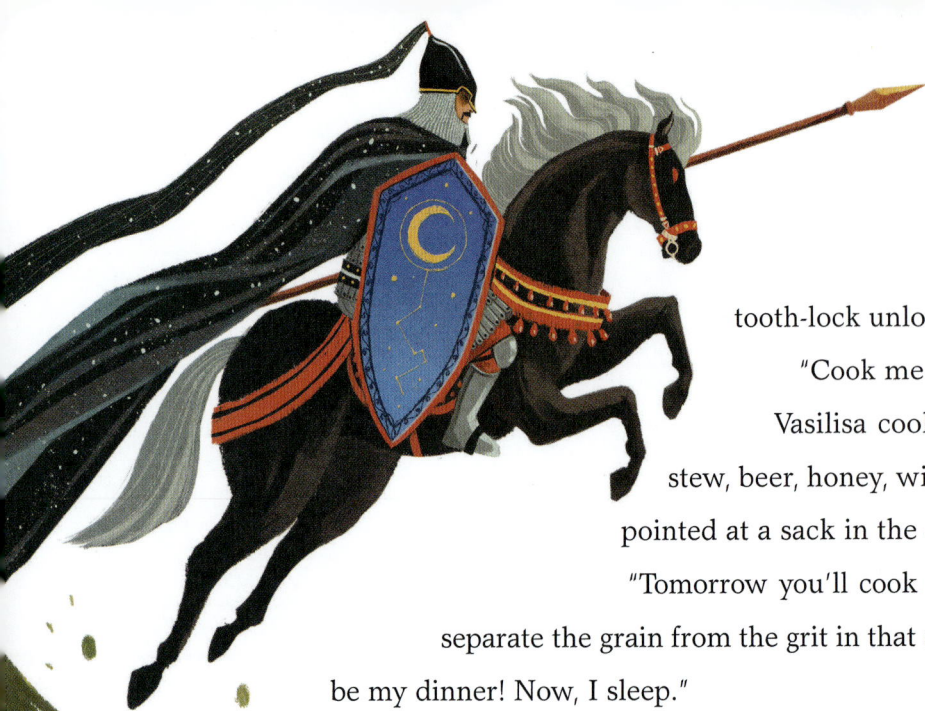

tooth-lock unlocked itself and they went inside.

"Cook me a meal!" Baba Yaga ordered.

Vasilisa cooked and Baba Yaga ate – bread, stew, beer, honey, wine – until she was full. Then she pointed at a sack in the corner.

"Tomorrow you'll cook my dinner, clean the house and separate the grain from the grit in that sack before I return – or you will be my dinner! Now, I sleep."

Baba Yaga's snores rattled the house, and Vasilisa wept. But then she remembered to feed the doll, who woke, ate, drank and advised, "Sleep now – the morning is wiser than the evening."

So Vasilisa slept, as the black horse rider and then the white thundered past the window.

Snap! Crack! Dawn. Baba Yaga was gone when Vasilisa woke, and the house was clean. The grain was separated from the grit and the doll was back in Vasilisa's pocket. All she had to do was cook, and she knew how to do that.

Snap! Crack! Baba Yaga was back! Bony leg clacking on the floor, she inspected the house.

"Hmm – well done. Tonight I'll eat bread and not you!"

The grain ground itself, kneaded itself into a loaf and baked itself in the oven. Baba Yaga ate, then she pointed at a jar on the shelf.

"As you did today, tomorrow you will cook, clean and separate seeds from gravel in that jar – or you will be my dinner!"

Baba Yaga slept and Vasilisa wept – but once again, the doll woke, ate, drank and then sang Vasilisa to sleep. Soon everything was done, and the next morning, the doll was just a doll again, safe in Vasilisa's pocket.

"Clever girl. Tonight I drink poppyseed oil, and not you!" cried Baba Yaga.

Magic hands pressed seeds into oil. Baba Yaga drank, then glared at Vasilisa

"Don't just stand there! You have shown intelligence. Ask me something, if you dare! And make sure it's a good question. Go on, speak!"

Vasilisa took a breath. "I've seen horses and riders in white, red and black go past the house – what are they?"

"Ha! Not bad. But think. Consider *when* you see them and you will have your answer. In this place, they are my servants. Daybreak, Sunrise and Nightfall. Obviously. Next question!"

"Why do you live deep in the forest, surrounded by dead things?"

"Ha! The forest is grandmother to all, girl! All life springs from what has passed away before it. And all owe life to what has died before," said Baba Yaga. "Next question!"

"Why do you fly around in a mortar? Why do you eat some people, but help others?"

"Within the ordinary is the extraordinary, my clever girl. Next question!"

But Vasilisa stood waiting, with her hand in her pocket. "No more questions, Grandmother. Time passes quickly enough."

"Well said!" Baba Yaga cackled, "One question more would have been death to you. But now, my turn. I ask YOU – how were you able to do the tasks I set you?"

Baba Yaga did not lie; neither did Vasilisa. From her pocket, she brought out the doll. "My mother made her for me, to help me when she was gone."

"Euuurgghh! Mother's blessing! Such a thing is not welcome here!"

But nevertheless, Baba Yaga picked one of the glowing-eyed skulls from her fence and threw it at Vasilisa, who caught it. "Your New Mother sent you for light – take this back to her and see how it warms her!"

The glowing-eyed skull knew the way, and with the little doll in her pocket, Vasilisa let the skull lead her from Baba Yaga's house to the edge of the forest towards home.

Rata and the Hakuturi
A Maōri tale

Maōri mythology is full of stories of the creation of the world, gods, goddesses and brave heroes. One such hero is Rata – the grandson of Tāwhaki, a demigod of thunder and lightning. Rata's own magical adventures happen in the magnificent island landscapes of the Southern Pacific ocean. This story features an encounter with the iconic Tōtara – a tall, straight tree, which only grows on the islands of Aotearoa, New Zealand – and some mischievous magical forest guardians.

Long ago, where snow-capped mountains and long coastlines meet mighty forests, Wahieroa, son of Tāwhaki, was kidnapped by the ogre Matukutakotako, and never seen again. When Rata, son of Wahieroa, came of age he vowed to find his father, travelling the whole of the land until he found Matukutakotako and destroyed him. But when he searched the ogre's lair, Wahieroa was gone: the *ponaturi* – sea goblins – had taken him far across the ocean.

"I must follow them!" said Rata. "But to conquer the waves and fight my enemies, I need a *waka* – a canoe – bigger than any ever seen before, carved from a single great tree, fit to carry 150 strong warriors."

Rata took an axe and walked to where the tallest, widest, straightest trees in the land grew: the forest of Tāne, God of Woodlands and Birds, and child of Sky Father Rangi and Earth Mother Papa.

Under the green shade of mighty trees, with twigs crunching under his feet, Rata walked until he came to the heart of the forest, where a great Tōtara tree stood, higher and straighter than seven tall men standing on each other's heads. So wide was it that it took Rata six long strides to get from one side to the other. Far above his head, the wind whistled in the huge tree's tiny leaves.

"Yes, this will be my *waka*," Rata said, and with his axe he began to CHOP, CHOP, CHOP until, finally, just before nightfall – TIMBER! – the tree fell – BOOM! – to the forest floor, and Rata went back to the village to rest.

Excited, Rata returned at daybreak. But when he arrived, he found that the tree was upright again!

"How?" puzzled Rata. "Some strange mischief, perhaps? No matter, I will fell it again." He cut the great tree down again, halved it lengthways and hollowed the inner heartwood into the shape of a canoe.

He worked past nightfall, returning to the village when the Moon was high in the sky. The forest of Tāne was silent behind him. But as soon as Rata was out of sight, the leaves shirred and rustled, and long lines of tree insects began to walk towards the felled tree. Above them, birds flew down from their treetop nests, singing night songs. Then other creatures emerged – bird-like, but not birds, tree-like, but not trees, and glowing green. They slid through the forest chanting in a whisper that grew louder and louder until they surrounded the fallen tree. The forest spirits, the insects, the birds raised their voices, and sang:

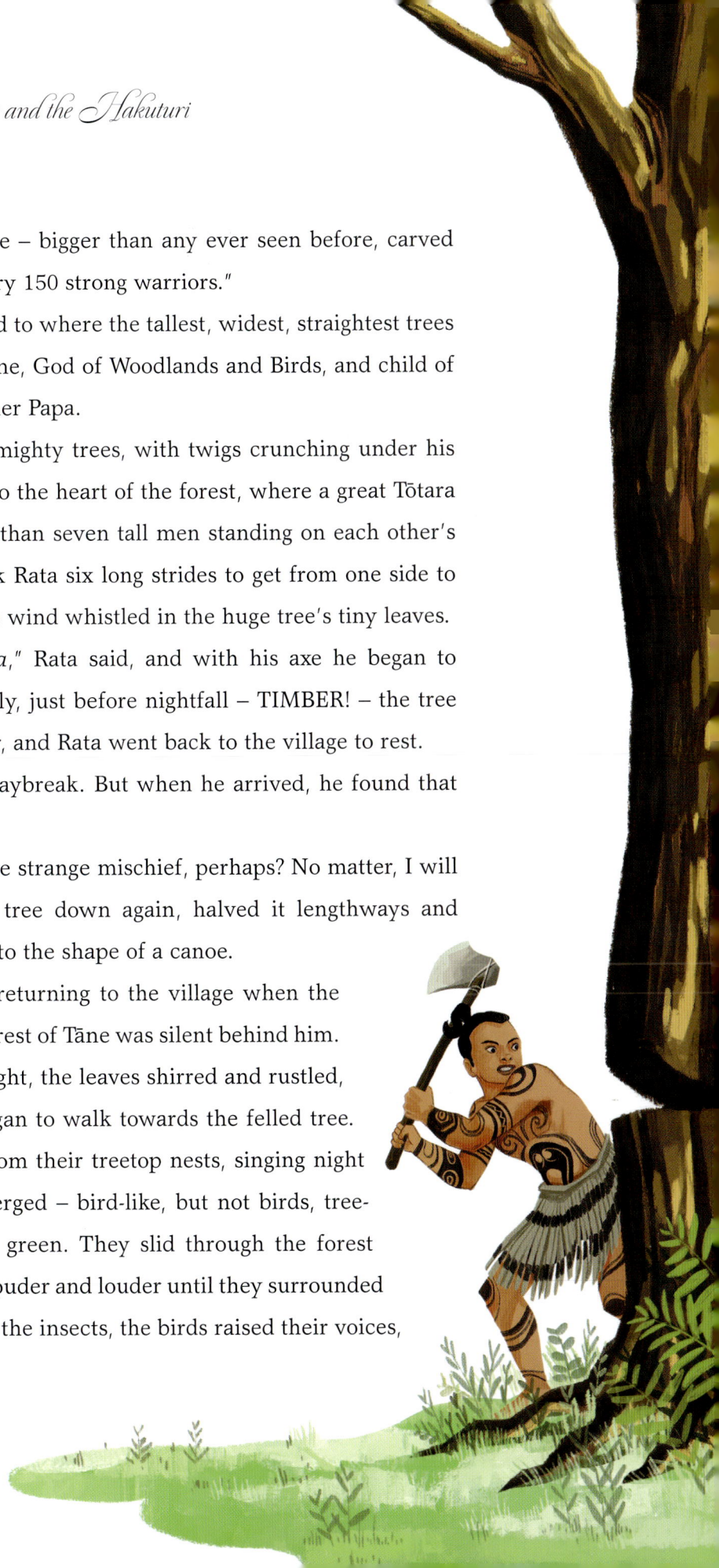

"As you stood before, may you stand again, Riwaru."

As they chanted, chip by chip, the great tree re-erected itself. Soon, it stood tall and magnificent once more, and the work was done. The forest creatures fell silent. The birds returned to their nests, and the insects returned to their leaves.

The next morning, when Rata found the tree standing again, he was angry.

"Why?! You are mine! I will fell you again. This time you will not rise up!"

For a third time, Rata cut down the tree and carved out the heartwood. Night fell, and Rata packed up his things. But instead of going back to the village, he hid, waiting and listening in the dark tree-shadows. Silence.

Then he saw rustling leaves, insects, birds and glowing green creatures surrounding the tree, whispering, chanting, singing words of healing. But just as the first wood chip returned to the tree, Rata sprang out!

"Stop! This tree is mine! With it, I'll build a mighty *waka* to sail across the sea! Who are you to stop me?"

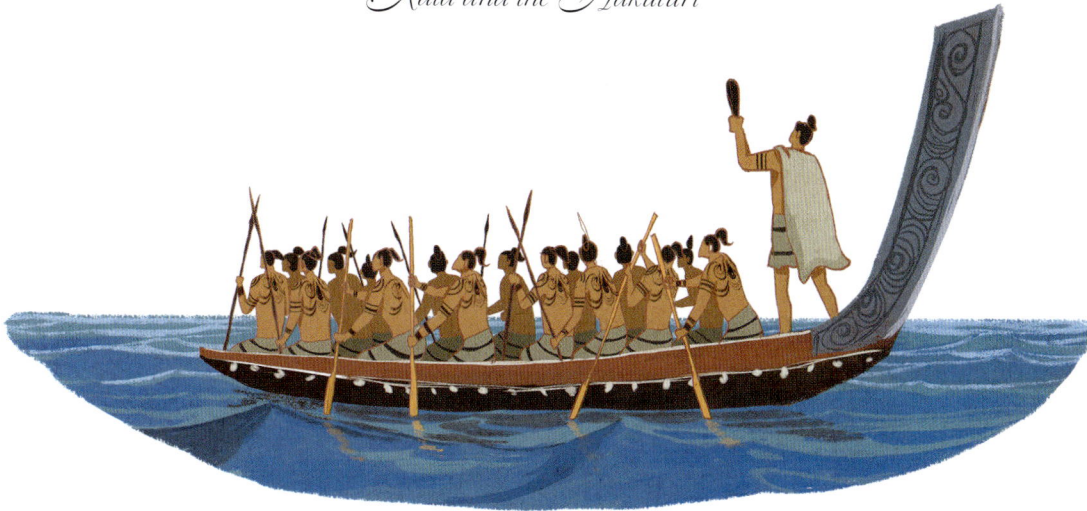

As one, thousands of pairs of glowing eyes turned on Rata and, as one, all the creatures spoke.

"YOUR tree?"

"My tree! I chose it! I need it!" Rata replied.

"No. You own nothing: you are a trespasser here. We are the Hakuturi, forest guardians and children of Tāne! Tāne decrees that every tree is its own master. This tree is Riwaru. To fell such a being without permission is to be a thief, just like your father's kidnapper!"

The Hakuturi's words pierced Rata's heart, and he was ashamed.

"I am truly sorry. I humbly beg permission to make Riwaru into the finest *waka* that ever sailed, to cross the sea and find my father!"

As one, the Hakuturi nodded. "You ask well, consent is granted. Go, we will craft this vessel tonight. Meet Riwaru on the sea shore at first light."

Rata obeyed, and the Hakuturi kept their word. At dawn, there on the shore was a *waka*, covered along its sides, and at prow and stern, with swirling carvings, patterns and stories from the dawn of time. It was the most magnificent *waka* Rata had ever seen.

In thanks, Rata held a ceremony for the *waka* whose name was Riwaru. Then, carrying 150 warriors, weapons and provisions, with space to spare, it slipped through the water like a sea turtle, towards the island of the *ponaturi*.

The Search for the Magic Lake
A tale from Ecuador

Water really is magic! It covers three-quarters of the world. It can easily turn from a solid into a liquid, then seem to disappear into the air. It helps plants grow, and keeps everything living alive. Water is the star of "The Search for the Magic Lake", an adventure which flies across the huge skylines, deep rainforests, bustling cities and lush farmlands of Peru and Ecuador.

When the son of the great Sun King fell mysteriously ill, the bright city of Cusco dimmed. Not even the best doctors in the land could cure the Prince, so the King sent for the best magicians. They built a fire, fed it with wood and gold, and asked the flames for their wisdom.

Crackle! Snap! The flames gave their answer. *The only cure is water from the magic lake at the top of the world!*

The flames died down, and in the glowing embers was an empty golden water flask, carved with ornate designs – reflections of the sun, a crab, a snake and a trail of tiny ants.

90

The King made a royal vow. "Whoever brings that water cure will forever be my family!"

To be part of the royal family was a great honour. All over the kingdom young men set off to search for the magic lake. But it was a dangerous journey, through steaming jungles full of pumas and giant snakes. Some who ventured never returned. Those that did found seas, rivers, mountains and volcanoes, but none found the magic lake.

Meanwhile, far from Cusco, on a farm where golden corn and white-haired llamas grew side by side, two brothers heard of the Sun King's decree and set off to try their luck, leaving their little sister Ayar behind. All spring and summer they searched, until one day, by another lake, they agreed it was time to go home for the harvest.

"But how can we go without the magic water?" said one of the brothers.

"We'll take some water from this lake! Who knows – it might be magic!" said the other.

The two brothers returned to Cusco with a jar of lake water and presented it to the King. But as he poured it into the golden flask, it evaporated.

"Liars! Cheats! Throw them in prison!" screeched the King.

The bad news travelled back to the brothers' farm, to their parents and their sister, Ayar.

"The Prince is ill and my boys are captured? What can we do?" cried their mother.

"There is only one choice – we must find the magic water," said Ayar. "Mother, father, you gather the harvest: I will go!"

Though she was young, Ayar was brave, and she was right: there was no other choice. She packed a bag with food for the journey and a jar for the water, and said goodbye to her parents. Ayer set off on her llama, towards the jungle and the mountains, under the huge blue sky.

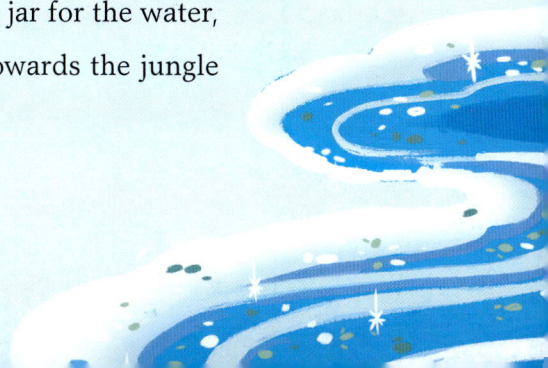

On the first night, Ayar slept under the stars beside her llama, warmed by its fluffy coat. But on the second day, she heard a jaguar's cry, so she climbed a tall tree, and freed the llama.

"Go home – be safe!" she cried.

Day became night. Ayar sat alone, and the world was big and strange. And noisy! In the branches above her sat three rainbow-feathered macaws, gossiping.

"Another magic water-seeker!" said one.

"She'll never find it alone!" said another.

"Should we help?" said the third.

"Let's see!" they cried.

The birds swooped down and landed on the branch beside Ayar. She shared her corn with them, and with nobody else to talk to, she told them everything.

"Oh, what a to-do! You gave gifts to us – we'll give gifts to you!" vowed the macaws. In a circle, each lifted its beak, pulled three feathers from the other, and placed them on the branch in a fan shape.

"This fan holds the magic of a bird's wing – for light-fast travel, for peaceful flights!" they chorused.

"Thank you!" Ayar picked the feathers up, closed her eyes and whispered, "Feather-fan, take me to the lake at the top of the world!"

Her eyes opened to sunlight dazzling on blue water and bouncing off mountain peaks. She was here!

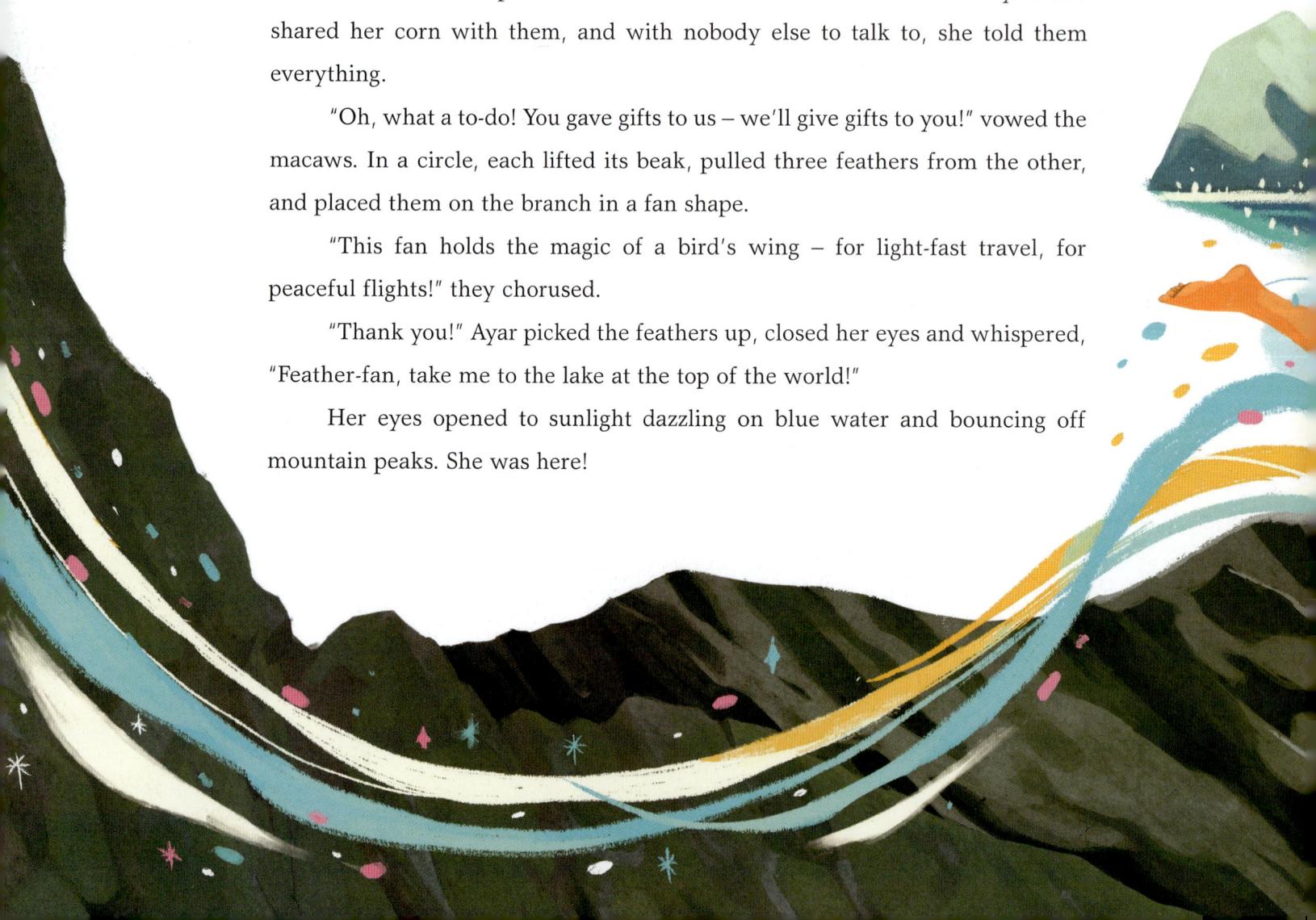

Ayar rushed to the shore with her water jar – then stopped. A huge, black claw broke the lake's surface, followed by another.

It was a crab, the size of a giant sea turtle.

"Who dares to take from MY lake?" it rasped.

The crab then shirred up the bank towards her, rustling the sand and grass behind it.

Ayar scrambled for her belt-knife, but her hand found the feather fan instead.

"Stop!" Ayar cried. She shut her eyes tight, crouched behind the feather fan and waited for the sting of sharp claws. But none came. Ayar opened her eyes – the crab had fallen softly to the sand fast asleep.

"Thank you, feather fan!" she breathed, and rushed back to the shore with the jar. But then, bubbling and simmering up from the lake shallows, came a giant emerald snake.

"Who dares to take from MY lake?" it hissed.

Ayar backed away and raised the feather fan.

"Stop, I mean no harm!" she said.

The snake swayed, coiled up and, like the crab, fell fast sleep.

Again, Ayar took the jar and approached the water... But rising to the surface was an army of thousands of sea ants. The ants swarmed over Ayar's hand and the jar and the feather fan, as if to carry them away. But Ayar would not let go. She raised up the fan, seething with the sea ants, and her voice carried far and loud.

"I mean no harm! I come in peace! This lake's water can cure the Prince of my country, and set my brothers free!"

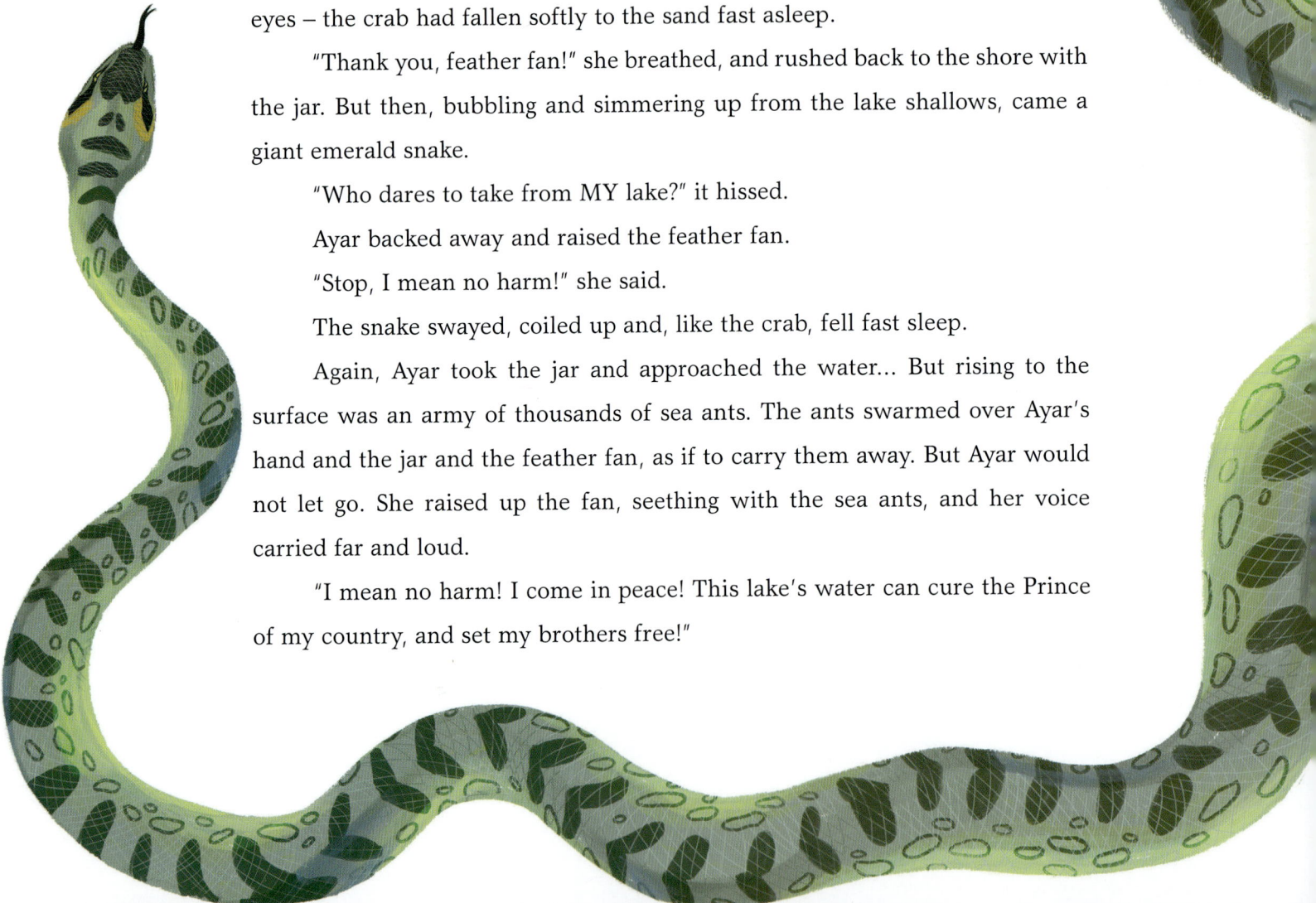

As one, the ants stopped as still as tiny seeds. And as one, they backed away and fell deeply asleep on the bank.

Ayar filled the jar of water, smiled at the sparkling lake's beauty, and breathed *"Thank you"* to the three lake guardians. Then she held up the fan.

"The Sun King's palace!" she cried.

The fan spread out, the lake disappeared, and suddenly Ayar was standing before the Sun King. She poured the water into the decorated golden flask, and when it did not evaporate, the King ordered it to be rushed to his son. As soon as the water touched the Prince's lips, he opened his eyes, and miraculously started to get well.

"Young woman, saviour! Who are you?" said the Sun King. "From this day forward, you are family, and shall have anything you desire!"

"Your Majesty, I am Ayar, and you honour me. But my two brothers are in your prison. All I want is for you to release them, and let us all go home to our farm."

"That's all?" he said, with a smile. "Very well."

That was how Ayar found the magic lake, saved the Sun King's heir, set her brothers free, earned a place in the King's family and returned home – with llamas laden with gifts that would last a lifetime, and stories to last forever.

Sources

Lotus Cloud Mountain
Retellings include "The Fairy Grotto" in *The Brocaded Slipper and other Vietnamese Tales* (HarperCollins: 1982), and "The Land of Bliss", in *Vietnamese Legends* (Tuttle: 1965). Special thanks to Quang and Lien who helped me choose this story.

Under the Iroko Tree
"The pot that boils over only dirties itself" appears in *Not Even God Is Ripe Enough: Yoruba Stories* collected by Ulli Beier and Bakare Gbadamosi (Heinemann:1968).

The Little Stars of Gold
This story appears in *The Disobedient Kids and other Czecho-Slovak fairy tales* collected by Božena Nemcová (Koci:1921), and shares similarities with "Die Sterntaler" recorded by the Brothers Grimm. I've renamed the heroine Magda, after a dear, brave friend.

The Twelve Dancing Princesses
First published in *Contes du Rois Cambrinus* (1874), Deulin's version is one of many stories of its "tale-type".

Sigurd and Fafnir
This story retells a popular episode from the Old Norse legendary Völsunga Saga, whose story inspired Tolkien's *Lord of the Rings* and Wagner's *Ring Cycle*.

The Magic Fish
Ye-Hsien/Ye-Tsien is found in many retellings, including *The Cinderella Story* by Neil Philip (Penguin, 1989). Its beginning is strikingly similar to Haitian folktale "Tayzanne" collected by Diane Wolkstein in *The Magic Orange Tree* (Knopf: 1978).

The Stonecutter
This story appeared in Andrew Lang's *Red Fairy Book* (1895) as "a story from Japan", but its origins seem to lie with a nineteenth-century Dutch writer creating a Japan-inspired take on the (European) "Fisherman's Wife" story-type. Its treatment of the natural world evokes values of Shinto and Buddhism (Japan's main religions); and the ending – a choice, not a punishment – is like a Zen parable. It's a reminder of how stories travel, change and grow roots in different landscapes.

Tom Tit Tot
One place this English cousin to Grimm tale "Rumpelstiltskin" appears, is Katharine Briggs's *British Folk Tales & Legends* (Routledge: 1977).

Oh, Tsar of the Forest
This tale is found in R. Nisbet Bain's *Cossack Fairy Tales and Folk Tales* (Lawrence & Bullen: 1894) and Bilenko's *Ukrainian Folk Tales* (Dnipro: 1974). In my version, the apprenticeship is slightly shortened, but the shape-shifting wizard fight is not!

The Dove Princess
"The Eagles" is a member of a family of "brothers turned into birds" tales, which includes "Twelve Wild Ducks" collected by Asbjørnsen and Moe in *Norwegian Folk Tales*, and Grimm tale *Seven Ravens*. My main source is A. J. Glinski's *Polish Fairy Tales* (Bodley Head: 1920), and online sources including surlalunefairytales.com.

The Foolish Brothers
"The Four Brothers Who Brought a Dead Lion to Life" was first recorded by Somadeva in his eleventh-century collection *Kathasaritsagara* (Ocean of Stories). Here, I've changed the lion into a tiger. Fascinating fact: a similar group of brothers use the same powers to bring their father back to life in West African folktale "Cow Tail Switch"!

The Star Husbands
My interpretation is woven from various sources, primarily Mi'kmaq legends "Women Who Married Star Husbands" and "Of the Surprising and Singular Adventures of Two Water Fairies", available at the firstpeoples.us website, and also in Lee's *Folk Tales of All Nations* (Harrap: 1931). I was also inspired by Ben Haggarty's *Mezolith 2* (Archaia: 2016) and an oral performance by Nell Phoenix.

Snow White
"Little Snow-white" appeared in the Grimms' 1812 first edition of *Childrens and Household Tales*. Various details were changed for later editions, including that the villain, originally Snow White's mother, became her stepmother. Wicked stepmothers are great story-characters – but in honour of my own (not-at-all wicked) stepmother, I have chosen to follow the first edition here.

The Bird of the Golden Feather
This story is retold by Gertrude Mittelmann in *The Bird of the Golden Feather and other Arabic Folktales* (Bell: 1969) and Inea Bushnaq in *Arab Folktales* (Penguin: 1987). My version slightly simplifies the plot, and tweaks the structure so Kassim can tell his own story.

Blodeuwedd
This story ends the fourth branch of the Mabinogion, first written down over 1,000 years ago and popularised by Lady Charlotte Guest's English translation in the 1840s. More recent versions include Sioned Davies's *Mabinogion* (OUP: 2007) and Sian Lewis's *Four Branches of the Mabinogi* (Rily: 2015).

The Doll and the Light
"Vasilisa the Beautiful" was collected by Alexander Afanasyev in the 1850s, and included in his landmark collection *Russian Fairy Tales*. My version is inspired by various English translations, and oral performances by Sarah Liisa Wilkinson, Kim Normanton and Vanessa Woolf.

Rata and the Hakuturi
I worked with versions found in *Maori Myths and Tribal Legends* by Anthony Alpers (Houghton Mifflin: 1966) and the online library of Victoria University of Wellington (NZ). Thanks also to Te Ara – Encyclopedia of New Zealand whose descriptions of Tōtara trees and *waka* helped bring my retelling to life.

The Search for the Magic Lake
Retellings appear in Ethel Johnston Phelps's *Tatterhood and Other Tales* (Feminist Press: 1978), Heather Forest's *Wonder Tales from Around the World* (August House: 1995) and online sources including https://storiestogrowby.org.

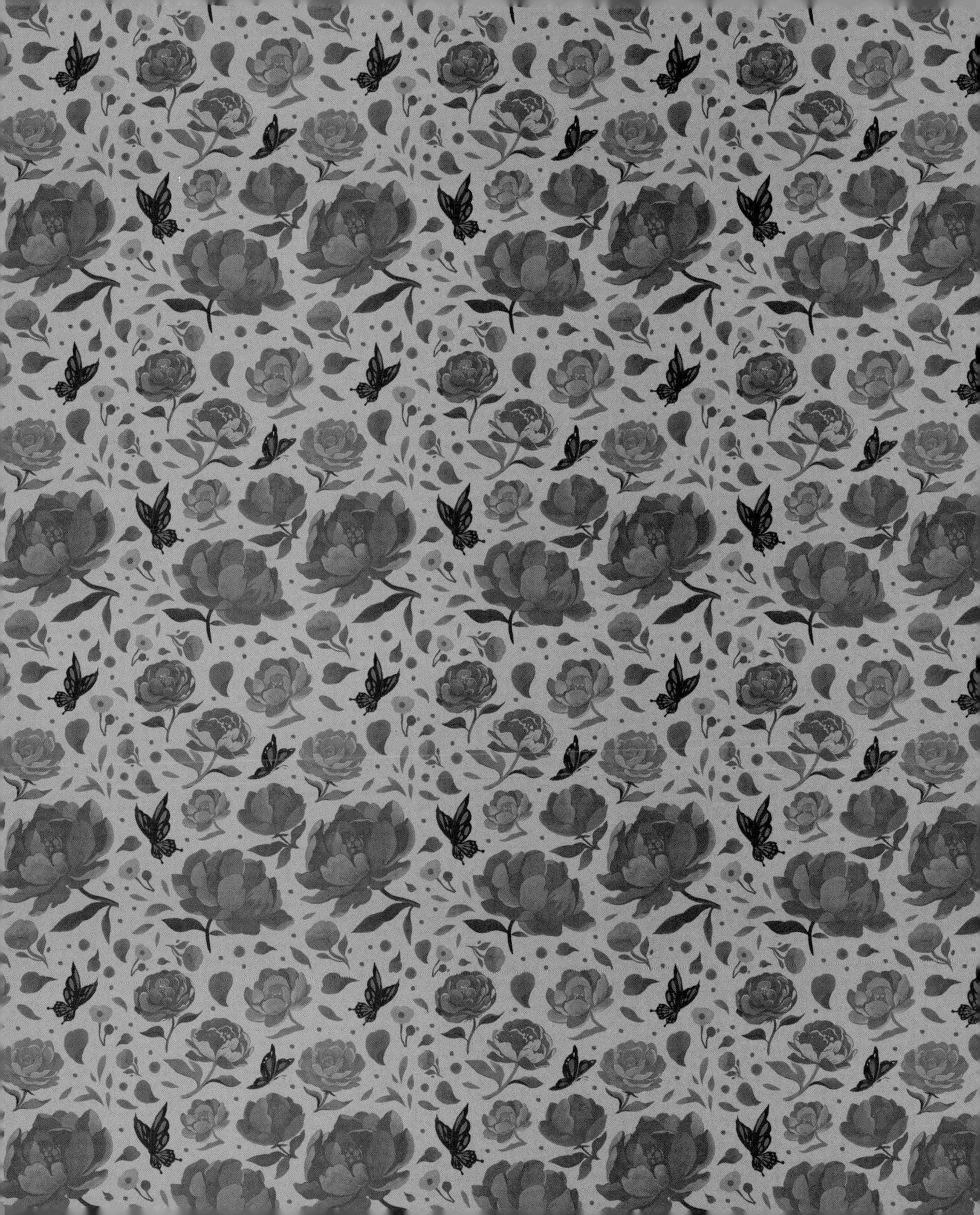

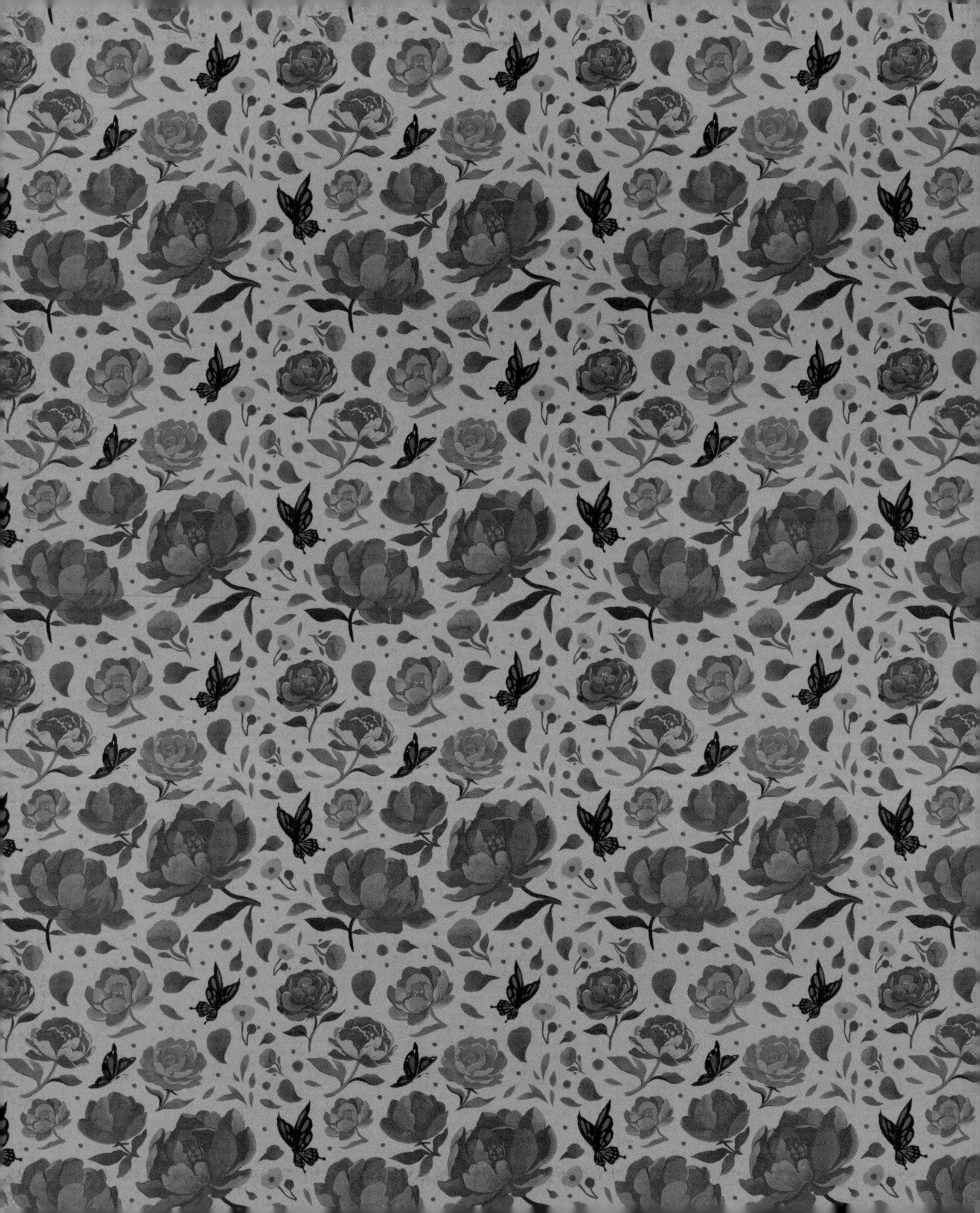